Read MY Shorts!

~a collection of my short stories, short shorts, and essays...

Melanie Young

Melanie Young

Copyright © Melanie Young 2011

Some of the selections in this book are works of fiction. Names, characters, places, and incidents either are the product of the author's imagination or are used fictitiously, and any resemblance to actual persons, living or dead, events, or locales is entirely coincidental.

ISBN 978-1-257-04723-9

Read MY Shorts!

Melanie Young

Read MY Shorts!

"I write to tell stories. I believe that there are some professions in the world that will last forever: doctor or a nurse, teacher, builder and a storyteller. I write also to become myself, more so day by day. Writing is a way to shape out visible and invisible, in myself as well as in the world."

~Eppu Nuotio

Melanie Young

To my wonderful friend, Marie McElen,
who always encourages to keep writing!

Melanie Young

Introduction

When I decided to put together a collection of my short stories in a book, I thought it would be an easy process. Don't get me wrong, it's not like it was difficult, but it was definitely a little more challenging than I thought. For one thing, not all of the stories I wanted to include were finished, and some of them I ended up rewriting several times (one of them I couldn't decided whether I wanted the story to be a little scary or a little humorous and kept starting it over every time I changed my mind). Another problem that I didn't expect was that I had a harder time deciding which stories to include and which to leave out, especially when it came to the essays that are in the book.

All of the stories, except the first one, "The Appointment in Samarra," were written by me. The essays are scattered among the stories but are in chronological order by the date they were originally written.

I want to say a special "Thank You" to my mother, Claire Bardwell, who does all my line editing. Thank You, Mom!!

Melanie Young

Contents

"The Appointment in Samarra"
(as retold by W. Somerset Maugham [1933])

This is my favorite short story…and I sought out Somerset Maugham literature after reading it in college, even writing a paper on him…

There was a merchant in Bagdad who sent his servant to market to buy provisions and in a little while the servant came back, white and trembling, and said, Master, just now when I was in the marketplace I was jostled by a woman in the crowd and when I turned I saw it was Death that jostled me. She looked at me and made a threatening gesture, now, lend me your horse, and I will ride away from this city and avoid my fate. I will go to Samarra and there Death will not find me.

The merchant lent him his horse, and the servant mounted it, and he dug his spurs in its flanks and as fast as the horse could gallop he went.

Then the merchant went down to the marketplace and he saw me standing in the crowd and he came to me and said, "Why did you make a threatening gesture to my servant when you saw him this morning?"

"That was not a threatening gesture," I said, "It was only a start of surprise. I was astonished to see him in Bagdad, for I had an appointment with him tonight in Samarra."

A Perfect Morning

I hope you have as much fun reading this story as I had writing it! It is my favorite of my short stories. I always enjoy watching someone read it, or even hearing it read aloud, because I like to see people's faces as the story unfolds....

It was the kind of morning you dream about. There were just a few fluffy white clouds in the lovely cyan colored sky. You could imagine jumping into the clouds and being enveloped in their softness. The sun was shining brightly and warming the earth in an ethereal calmness. A slight breeze rustled through the trees and carried the early summer fragrances, stirring the air. Birds sang softly in a splendid serenade.

Hannah had been sleeping so peacefully on her bed, and woke up to the glorious sun shining through the bedroom window, opening her beautiful brown eyes slowly, blinking herself fully awake. She was glad the blinds were open so she could soak up the sun's fabulous glow. Her gorgeous flowing auburn hair glistened in the golden sun. She felt wonderful! She was well rested, and seeing that it was a beautiful morning made her ecstatic. This was the perfect kind of morning that made her so happy to be alive! Hannah yawned and leisurely stretched, relishing the lovely morning, wondering when Jack had gotten up, and how he managed to do so without waking her.

Getting out of bed, Hannah stretched again and walked over to the glass slider that led out to the deck, and overlooked the expansive backyard. The redwood deck spanned the length of the house and they often had company over for barbecues. She loved this home, especially the magnificent backyard. The landscaping looked like it had been professionally done, although Jack had done it all himself. It had been wonderful when he had been working on the yard. Although Hannah couldn't help with the work, they had spent many hours together as he was doing the work. He had really put a lot of love and effort into making this house a home for them. Hannah yawned and stretched again, feeling wonderfully lazy on this fabulous morning. She walked through the house looking for Jack. There were no sounds from the television, so he obviously wasn't watching the news in the family room. Thinking he might be reading the morning paper in the sun room, she checked there. He might be eating or preparing breakfast, but when she looked in the kitchen and dining room he was not there. Jack was nowhere to be seen. All of a sudden her morning was not perfect! Jack had left. Had he gone to work, when he had promised to spend the day with her? Jack had given his word that they would go to the lake today since he had been working so much. They had no time to spend together lately. She felt really let down. Jack shattered her mood. She was instantly depressed.

Now Hannah didn't know what to do; she had so been looking forward to their outing to the lake. She wandered around the house aimlessly, and ended up at the back door. She might as well benefit from the sun so she went out onto the back deck and stretched some more in the warmth of the sun. She tried not to think of how nice it would be to be driving to the lake right now, or how refreshing it would be to swim in the lake, or how fun it would be to play with Jack on the beach. Hannah was really fraught with this depression that Jack had forced on her this morning. She felt like he had abandoned her. Walking around the yard, Hannah glanced at the fabulous gazebo Jack had built last summer. What a waste! He was never here to enjoy it! He promised he wasn't going to work so hard anymore, and that they would spend the day at the lake together. Where had he gone? How could he break his promise again? She just wasn't going to think about it.

Hannah walked the border of the yard, soaking up the sunshine. This yard had become her private paradise. The corner of the yard had been dedicated to a lovely flower and herb garden, with a wood and wrought iron bench in the center. There amongst the flowers, she noticed a butterfly and wandered over to watch it. It was a majestic Monarch butterfly, fluttering from one flower to another, not landing on any of them. Hannah sat down and watched the butterfly, getting lost in the gracefulness of the creature. Hannah closed her eyes, and relaxed in the warmth of the sun's rays, turning her face up to claim as much of the heat as she could. It was a beautiful morning.

Suddenly, Hannah heard a vehicle pull up to the house. Was that Jack's pickup? "Hannah!" It was Jack! Hannah ran for the house and through the dog door as fast as her legs could carry her. "Are you ready to go to the lake, girl?" Hannah, a gorgeous Irish Setter, jumped up with her front paws on Jack's chest and licked his face. It was a perfect morning.

Alice in Doll Land

*I wrote this story for a "24-hour short story contest". This contest takes place every 3 months. I receive the topic by email and have 24 hours in which to write the story and submit it. This was the first story I wrote for one of these contests. I wasn't home at the time the topic was sent because I was in Stuart, FL attending the annual "BookMania" at the Stuart Library and lucky enough to meet author Claire Cook, author of **Must Love Dogs**, while there. I think it took me longer to formulate an idea for the story based on the topic than it did to actually write it...*

From her lap, his shiny black eyes stared up at her as she admired his permanent red smile. Alice was proud of her lifelike clown doll creation. Fingering his tiny overalls, she could almost imagine him coming to life to entertain the children at the Sisters of Our Father Orphanage where she would be donating the dolls. The last strand of hair was finally in place on this last doll. She had fondly named this one Bonzo. She would deliver the dolls the next day, and hoped the orphans would delight in them as much as she did. As she gently tied the last knot, the phone rang, and Alice set the clown aside to walk across the room to where she had left her cordless phone.

The phone caller was only a telemarketer, but Alice was too polite to hang up on the person on the other end of the line. He was, after all, just trying to make a living. She finally convinced the man she didn't need to switch her auto insurance since she had neither a car nor insurance, and set the phone down. Alice sat back down in her chair and started to pick the clown doll back up from the table where she had laid him, when she realized he wasn't there. She was so sure she had set him on the table and stood up to look for him, when she heard what sounded like a footstep behind her. Alice turned and saw the doll standing up and looking up into her eyes.

This startled Alice, and she nearly fell backward. The corners of the doll's mouth curled up into a crazy and chilling grin. Alice couldn't move. Suddenly the doll started walking toward her, and he grew taller with each step he took. Alice screamed and ran in the other direction. Bonzo followed her across the room, and she ran down the hall tripping over a throw rug and falling to the floor. She turned her head to see the clown doll was still coming closer. Quickly rising, she ran further down the hall. Just as she neared the guest room door, where she was storing the finished clown dolls, she saw the door knob turning.

Alice screamed again, her heart was racing so fast she thought it would beat right out of her chest. How could her fun little dolls, which were created from her own heart and hands, have come to life? Would they actually harm her? She should have run for the door to get out of the house instead of down the hall. She was trapped, with no place to go but up the stairs. Hearing the steps behind her, she was afraid to turn around. She was at the end of the hall, and the door to the stairs stood before her.

Opening the door quickly, Alice stepped onto the stairs slamming the door behind her. She had just stepped onto the top step, when she heard a maniacal laugh and the door opened. She turned slightly to see what was happening before she ran from the staircase. She saw the dolls she had so lovingly crafted chasing her, with Bonzo in the lead. Alice ran down the upstairs hallway. The clown dolls' footsteps sounded like marching soldiers as they followed her. She was shaking badly and started to cry.

Alice got to the end of the hallway, and ran into the bathroom, locking the door behind her. She could hear those menacing steps coming closer, and was completely panicked knowing there was nowhere for her to go. Surely, clown dolls can't get through a locked door! Suddenly she heard that sinister laugh again, and could see they were trying the doorknob. Alice cringed into the corner, and the dolls started banging on the door. She hugged herself trying to control her shaking and cowered further into the corner, crying as the banging grew louder and louder.

"Open up, Alice!"

The banging continued.

"Alice, are you there?"

Alice slowly woke up, a little dazed, looking cautiously around the room. She could hear someone knocking on her front door. Then she heard the voices of her friends calling, "Alice, are you there?" She was hugging Bonzo tightly to her chest.

Letter to Amy

This was an assignment when I was a junior in high school. Anyone who went to Colville High School in the 1980's was in Ms. Carolyn Chase's class for English and/or history classes. In this particular assignment, Ms. Chase read a letter aloud to us (or maybe one of the students in the class read it), and I regret to admit that I do not remember anything about the letter, or who wrote it, although I do believe it was a famous author. As I remember the assignment was to write a letter to someone younger than us giving advice. I have kept this letter all these years. It's obvious that I was a typical teenage girl, and had apparently been through some recent drama. This letter is to my niece, Amy, my oldest brother's daughter. I have kept everything as it was in 1981; expect some weird punctuation and sentence structure. The original paper is quite yellowed with age. Warning…it's corny!

March 19, 1981

Dear Amy,

I'm writing this letter to you to tell you about life. The reason I'm doing this is because I've been alive almost 17 years longer than you. So I probably know a little more about it than you do. One thing you should always remember is that life can be good to you if you are good to life; and to yourself. Always get the best out of live that you can. Live it to its fullest.

Never let life get you down, Amy; because if you do, it's awful hard to get back up again. It's like a big wind has knocked you down. It's so strong that it's pushing you farther and farther until you're so low that you think you can never get up. If you ever get that low, Amy, fight. Fight with all you have. Reach for something and pull yourself up.

When life gets you down, remember that things could always be worse. A depressing, but true thought is that things will probably get worse before they get better. Don't ever worry about it, though, because when they get better, they'll be a lot better! Then you'll forget there was ever anything wrong. Life will be great again and you'll be happy. I saw a poster once that said, "If life gives lemons, make lemonade." That's what

I want you to do, Amy. If everything seems sour and depressing, make the best of it.

You should have a good life, though, because you have a family that loves you and cares for you. Your parents may not have a lot of money, but they can give you more riches than what money can buy. They can give you more love than you will ever realize. When you have that much love, even the bad things don't seem so bad. Remember, Amy, that they will love you forever and give you the best life has to offer. I'll close now with one last statement: although you're only one week old today, you already have the best thing in life.

Love,

Your Aunt,

Melanie

By the way, I received 19 out 20 points for this assignment, with a "really nice letter" comment from the teacher. Oh, and at the time of publication, Amy still has never read this letter. She is now 30 years old.

Locked Out

I didn't know exactly where this story was going when I started it, but my characters always figure that out for me. ☺

Peter walked up behind Cindy and kissed the nape of her neck, "I'll be back in about five or six hours. Will you be alright without me, darling?" Peter had to drive into town for a meeting at his architectural firm, and when he returned they would have two weeks alone at their cabin on the lake.

The cabin was a three bedroom daylight ranch style log home. It was the largest home on the lake, with over 2,600 finished square feet. It had been difficult to justify holding on to the place as it was really too large for the three or four weeks they were able to spend there every year, but it had been in Peter's family for decades. So they felt the need to keep it in the family after Peter's parents both died in a car accident several years earlier. Peter's parents had lived in the home after their retirement, and had not updated the 1950's home. However Peter and Cindy had just finished a fabulous remodel, because they had hopes of spending more time there since they had now started their family. It was secluded enough for privacy and quiet, yet not so far from things that they felt isolated.

"Of course I will, silly. I have plenty to keep me busy with unpacking our bags and taking care of the baby. I might take a walk with Emma. It's so relaxing to just sit by the lake. I have my cell phone if anything comes up, and the signal is great here. But I will miss you!" Cindy hugged him tight and gave him a kiss that she knew would make him hurry back as soon as the meeting was over. She wished he didn't have to go but she was happy they would have two wonderful weeks to enjoy together at their cabin.

Peter sighed and told her, "You're making it hard for me to leave, you know."

"I know. That's my intention. I want to make sure you are back here as soon as you can be" she said as she released him, winked and gave him her sexiest smile. "You better get going! You're going to be late."

Peter gave her one last quick kiss and walked out the door. He stepped into his BMW X5, turned the key and the engine purred to life. It was an hour drive back to the city, and the scenery was gorgeous. It was a pleasant drive, but he was anxious to get the meeting done and over with so he could get back to Cindy and Emma. Emma was nearly six months old and this was their first vacation since they found out Cindy was pregnant. Peter was going to make sure they got away more often after this. Now that his firm was well established he knew that would be possible. His beautiful wife and new child were the reason he had worked so hard all these years, and he was glad all his hard work had paid off and he would be able to spend time with his family.

Cindy looked at Emma in her playpen, joyfully reaching for her toes, not quite able to hold onto them. "My sweet, sweet Emma...you are so fascinated by your toes. You're momma's good baby, precious angel." Cindy poured a cup of coffee and took a sip. "I think we should go sit on the deck for a while. It's such a lovely morning and the fresh air will be good for both of us."

Cindy opened the door leading out to the deck and brought her coffee out to the table before she walked back inside to pick up Emma. She picked her up, wrapping her in a soft blanket and laid her in the stroller. Cindy pushed the stroller out to the deck, closing the door behind her. Walking over to the table, she set the brakes on the stroller before sitting down to relax and savor her coffee and the morning. This end of the deck overlooked the lake and with the sun reflecting off the lake and the birds singing in the trees, it was exceptionally peaceful. Cindy thought about how perfect their life had become. She and Peter had been so happy in their marriage for seven years, and now that Emma was with them, they were truly a family. The world is so perfect for me right now. I am a lucky woman. She sipped her coffee, enjoying the magnificent morning as the sun warmed the earth. Emma cooed softly as Cindy gently caressed her cheek. Cindy thought she should unpack their bags soon and give Emma a bath before feeding her. After Emma's bath it would be nice to take a walk around the lake...the sling or the back pack? ...hmm... the sling I think. It was impossible to be stressed when she was at the lake house.

Cindy looked out over the lake. The water was very still this morning and looked like a mirror reflecting the tops of the trees and the few clouds. There was a gentle breeze, and the air was just cool enough that she needed her light jacket, but the glistening sun suggested it would warm up later. She saw a fish jump and watched the mellow ripples it made. It was such a peaceful morning.

Emma started to fuss, just as Cindy was finishing her coffee. "It must be time for your bath, sweet princess. You're momma's precious little girl." Cindy set down her coffee cup and picked Emma up, kissing her repeatedly as Emma squealed with delight and smiled at her mother's touch. Cindy reached for the doorknob and when it didn't turn, she realized she hadn't unlocked the door before she came out. Cindy felt an instant panic. Did we put the new keys under the rock after the new doors were installed? Peter won't be back for at least 4 hours. My cell phone! It's not in my pocket! Cindy walked down the steps and checked under the rock where the spare keys were always hidden. Damn...the old keys are still here!

I suppose I will just walk to the Murphy's house and wait for Peter...but they might not even be there by the time I get there. The closest neighbor was about a 45-50 minute walk. The weather was absolutely beautiful, so that seem like issue, but Emma needed to have her diaper changed and she would be hungry soon. I might be able to get one of the windows open and get in that way. Cindy tried the kitchen window first, and when it didn't budge, she tried the dining room window, the laundry room window, bedroom window, and realized that was useless. They had locked the place up tight last fall, and hadn't been back until they arrived last night. None of the windows had been opened; it was still somewhat cool, and there had been no need to open any windows.

Just then the weather began to change and the wind started to blow, and Cindy noticed storm clouds coming up over tops of the trees to the east. "Where did those clouds come from? I can't believe this. It was so beautiful and now that I realize I've locked us out of the house, the weather takes a turn." Cindy realized she was talking out loud. "And now to top it all off, I am acting like a crazy person."

Emma was really fussing now, and she had to do something soon. Why didn't I remember to unlock that stupid door before I closed it? I can't believe my cell phone isn't in my pocket...where is it anyway? We are idiots for not putting the new keys under that rock! Cindy was feeling frantic. I used to be able to open the basement door even when it was locked before we had the new doors installed. Prior to the remodel, the basement door didn't latch right, and it could easily be opened whether locked or not. Cindy almost wished they had not done the remodel because then she would easily be able to get in the house. She picked Emma up again and looked into her eyes.

She had to figure out a way to get into the house soon, the rain was more than just a sprinkle and it was picking up steadily. The wind was getting more blustery, and the air definitely felt chillier. Cindy had never known the weather to change so quickly like this. She might have to just break a window, and they could just get it repaired later. She started to look for a rock to break the window.

Cindy suddenly remembered something she hadn't thought of earlier! "Oh, Emmie, your mommy is so silly!" Cindy recalled that Peter had built a fire this morning in the wood stove in the basement, just to take the chill off the house, and had brought the firewood in through the basement door. It was likely he hadn't locked the door after carrying in the wood. She walked around the house and down the steps to the basement door. She grasped the knob and turned; the door opened easily.

Melanie Young

The Conference

This was fun story for me to write. I hope it's as fun for you to read!

I left the conference early and found a coffee shop down the street. I hate these conferences. They're always full of boring information I already know. In fact, I could teach the presenters a few things. My boss always insists that I go to these ridiculous things. My friends tell me I should take advantage of a couple of days off work and a free trip. It's not my idea of a good time!

In the first place, the conferences are always in some stupid large city that I've never had a desire to see. It always meant that I have to take a plane. I absolutely hate that! It's not that I'm afraid of flying. It's just that I don't like being crammed in like a can of sardines with a bunch of strangers. I always seem to get stuck next to the passenger who has a terminal case of diarrhea of the mouth, or worse, a plenitude of noxious gas.

Secondly, I never know anyone at these abhorrent seminars. I'm not an extroverted personality. It's not that I'm a boring person, or that I'm not fun. It's just that I am painfully shy. I'm not one of these people who can strike up a conversation with someone I don't know. So unless someone talks to me, I never have anyone to talk to. The cities they pick for the conventions are never the ones where I have friends. Even in the off hours, I am alone.

Some people at the conferences go to dinner with others they know at the conference, or they meet new people and go have drinks. Not me. I don't know anybody there, nor do I meet anybody. I spend the days sitting alone listening to some monotone speaker drone on and on, speaking on a subject about which I already consider myself an expert. Then I spend the evenings eating a lonely dinner in the hotel restaurant, followed by a lonely walk outside, and topped off with a lonely night of boring television in my hotel room. I'll say it again, I hate these conferences. I mean, I REALLY hate these conferences.

This particular afternoon, I decided that if my boss was going to be so ludicrous as to go to the expense of sending me to a conference filled with information I already knew, I was going to take the initiative to take my time into my own hands and spend some of it in a way of my own

24

choosing. I wasn't going to be a prisoner of the conference organizers. I would spend the afternoon doing whatever I wanted. I ducked out of the seminar shortly before they broke for lunch, avoiding the cattle chute the rest of the detainees would experience when they left for the noon meal.

I went for a walk along the waterfront. It was a pleasant walk. The weather was a little cloudy and windy, but it wasn't too cold. In fact with my light jacket and scarf, it was almost perfect. The fresh air was glorious and was certainly an improvement to the overly air conditioned atmosphere inside the conference room where people were coughing all over each other, sharing germs with everyone around them.

I noticed a vender selling bread crumbs to feed the ducks. I walked over to get some. Who spends $5.00 on a little bag filled with stale bread? Well, I suppose I do because before I knew it, I was tossing the tiny morsels to the ducks. I enjoyed watching them scrap for the small nuggets as if they were starving and that little crumb of bread was going to keep them from succumbing to their starvation. That is...I enjoyed it until some obnoxious goose decided she didn't like me and flapped her wings wildly, attacking me and beating my head and upper torso with her wings. I screamed and ran, dropping the rest of the bread crumbs.

I ran about two blocks before I realized the goose wasn't chasing me and I didn't need to keep running. I laughed at myself for being s frightened of a silly goose. I thought I shouldn't go too far from the hotel so as not to get lost. Once again, they had placed the conference in a city I wasn't familiar with. Fortunately by walking along the waterfront, I had guaranteed that I would be able to find my way back. Unfortunately, the peaceful clouds had turned into rain clouds and it began to rain, softly at first, but quickly becoming a downpour.

I ducked into a coffee shop to get out of the weather just before the downpour started. But then it really became a torrential rain and I marveled at my luck. I remembered that I hadn't eaten lunch yet, and I ordered a sandwich with my coffee. I sat next to the window to wait for my lunch watching the afternoon storm, and my sandwich arrived quickly. I had eaten about half my sandwich when I noticed a man, dressed all in black, watching me.

The man looked to be Cuban. He was dark; dark hair, dark skin, dark eyes, dark clothing. He saw that I noticed him and he picked up a magazine. I think he was only pretending to read it because his eyes kept coming back to me. I couldn't finish my lunch because the dark man was making me so nervous. I was almost more comfortable when he was openly watching me than when he pretended not to be.

I sat by that window watching the rain, waiting for a break in the clouds, so I could make a break and escape the dark man's watch. I went back and forth between watching the clouds and watching my "watcher". At one point, he glanced at his watch and then he pulled a cell phone from his jacket pocket and made a quick call before putting it back. I saw that he watched me during the call. Was he talking about me? Could it be that my stalker ex-boyfriend had hired a P.I.? Who was this dark man? I was probably just letting my imagination get away with me.

Finally it stopped raining. The clouds separated, leaving a small patch of blue sky. Now was my chance. I quickly walked out of the café leaving half my sandwich and coffee behind, as well as my watcher. I started down the waterfront. After I walked about thirty feet, I realized I was going in the wrong direction so I turned around just as the dark man, my watcher, walked out of the café door. I saw him look around, seemingly looking for something…or someone. Was he looking for me? Then he walked straight toward me. My heart started pounding and I turned around again, walking quickly in the opposite direction. As I was walking, I told myself that I was being silly and that this man wasn't following me, but when I turned slightly, I could see that he was indeed still behind me. His long legs were carrying him much faster than I could walk, and he was quickly gaining on me.

I ran into an open doorway, and watched from the shadows as he walked past. I stepped back out the door a few minutes later and walked quickly the other way, looking back repeatedly to make sure he wasn't behind me. Even though he was never there, I kept looking back just in case. It's a good thing I kept checking because all of a sudden I looked back and there he was running up behind me, "There you are," I heard him say. Now there was no doubt in my mind that he was following me, and I took off running again. Who was this dark man and what did he want from me? "Stop running!" He shouted.

There was no way I was going to stop running! I wished I hadn't left the conference. I turned a corner and slunk down behind some trash cans, praying that he couldn't hear my heart beating out of my chest, not to mention my breathing which had grown louder with each step. My watcher ran past me. I waited until I couldn't hear his steps anymore and cautiously came from behind the trash cans looking both ways. When I was sure he was out of sight I ran in the opposite direction. I was thoroughly lost now. I had apparently gotten myself into a bad section of the city because everyone I saw looked scary. Where were all the cops? Suddenly I ran directly into someone. We both nearly fell to the ground as he had been running also. It was the dark man! I turned and ran so fast I almost ran into a fence. I was able to sidestep the fence and ran past it.

"Lady, stop running! I have…" That's all I could hear as a truck went past me on the street. I crossed the street dodging cars and hoping to lose him. I had no idea where I was and how I would find my way back. I had no idea if I was going to live through this terrible ordeal. My heart was beating so fast, I would surely die of a heart attack if my watcher didn't kill me first. My throat was so dry it felt like it was on fire. I had to find a place to hide or I'd surely collapse and then he would have me.

I turned a corner allowing me to look back and I saw that he was far enough behind that I took the few seconds to try the next door I came to. It was locked. I kept running, but tried the next door and it opened. I ran inside, but saw the dark man before the door closed as I looked back. I could only hope he didn't see me. It was dark, but I could see that it was a stairwell. I wished I hadn't chosen this door to open, but I didn't want to take my chances by opening that door and possibly running into my watcher again. I started climbing the stairs. I had reached the top of the first flight, and heard the door open and daylight filled the stairwell. "Lady, are you here?"

I screamed. I couldn't help myself. It always makes me angry when horror movie heroines scream, and yet I screamed. I started running up the steps. "Lady, stop running from me." I couldn't hear what he yelled after that because all I could hear now was both of our footsteps on the stairs and the sound of my own heartbeat. I knew if I made it out of this predicament alive, I would never leave a conference again.

I felt like I would die as I reached the top of the stairwell. I knew I couldn't keep running and I didn't know what I would do if the door didn't open when I reached the top. As I got closer to the door, my fear that the door was locked grew. I was now at the top and I turned to look down. I could hear the dark man running up the stairs, "Lady…" I didn't wait any longer, and reached for the door knob and turned. The door stuck for a moment and then I pushed it open. My watcher obviously didn't know my name, so he wasn't a P.I. hired by my stalker ex-boyfriend. That meant that he was probably a serial killer or rapist.

As I stepped out onto the roof, I couldn't believe my eyes. I had no way out. There was a chain link fence all around me, and as I looked up, I saw that the fence had a roof. I was in a cage! I tried the gate, but it was locked solid. For the first time, I realized I didn't have my purse. I left it back at the café and my cell phone was in my purse. I looked around me to see if there was anything I could put against the door to keep the dark man from opening it. But there was nothing, except a three foot long two by four. My plan was to hit him with the board and try to knock him out and run back down the stairs.

I stood in a strategic spot in order to get the best swing. The door flung open suddenly and I took a swing with my board. My watcher held my purse up to block the swing. Wait minute…what was he doing with my purse. "Leave me alone!" I yelled. "Don't hurt me!" I started to take another swing. "Lady, what are you talking about? I'm not trying to hurt you." He grabbed the board out of my hands. "I saw that you left your purse in the café and I've been trying to catch you to give it to you. Didn't you hear me yell to you? I was telling you that I had your purse."

We were both breathing heavily. "I didn't hear what you were saying," I said sheepishly. "But why were you watching me in the café?" I was still panting.

"I'm sorry," My watcher said. "That was rude of me. It's just that you look exactly like my friend who I lost contact with several years ago. At first I thought you were her, and when I realized you weren't, I was trying to decide whether I should approach you anyway."

"You made a phone call…and you were watching me while you talked…were you talking about me?"

"What? Oh, I was calling…"

I continued to interrogate my dark watcher as we walked down the stairs together. When we finally reached the bottom, we were both terribly exhausted and we decided to go for a drink. My watcher didn't look scary anymore, he looked incredibly dreamy. My horrific nightmare had become an absolute dream.

I love going to conferences.

Letter to Mom and Dad

The following is a letter that I wrote to my parents after both my sons were born. Although the letter was to both of them, I gave it to them at breakfast on Mother's Day.

May 10, 1987

Mom and Dad,

I want to thank you for being my parents; and for being such good parents.

Thanks for helping me to grow by allowing me to do and experience the things you allowed me to do (even though it worried you- thanks for worrying.) Thanks for not allowing me to do the things I wanted so badly to do, but weren't necessary for my growth as a person – and wouldn't have been good for me. Thanks for helping me learn that I wouldn't "just die" if I couldn't do those things.

Thanks for teaching me right from wrong. Thanks for teaching me that when you do wrong, there are always consequences to pay – whether you get caught or not.

Thanks for giving me your opinions about things. Thanks for not forcing your opinions on me, but allowing me to have my own.

Thanks for all the advice and support you gave, and continue to give.

Thanks for being there when I needed you. Thanks for giving me space when I needed it.

Thanks for putting up with my temper over the years. Thanks for not knocking me through the wall all those times I slammed my bedroom door.

Thanks for letting me get into Rick and Ron's wrestling matches. Thanks for sympathizing when I got hurt.

Mom, thanks for nursing me for a year when I wouldn't take a bottle. (I can really appreciate that now – and sorry!)

Dad, thanks for teaching me to take care of my own car. (I really loved my Dodge!)

Mom, thanks for teaching me to cook and sew – even if it did cause us to fight.

Thanks for sharing your memories with me. But mostly, thanks for giving me so many happy memories to look back on.

I know that none us are "perfect," but I think we turned out pretty good – with your help. None if your children turned out to be drug addicts, prison inmates, psychopaths, communists, or politicians. (5 of the worst things I can imagine.)

I want you to know that you were, and are appreciated. Although I always appreciated you, (even though I didn't always act like it), now that I'm a parent myself, I appreciate you all the more.

For all the times I forgot, or just neglected, to say it…

THANKS!!!!!

I love you both!

Melanie

Regarding the "wrestling matches," Rick and Ron are my two older brothers and when I was a toddler, I got into the middle of their wrestling matches, always getting hurt. I didn't want to feel left out, but although they were gentle with me, I was fairly fragile (or so I thought – or maybe, I was just a big cry baby) and was easily hurt.

Cougar in a Red Dress

This is another entry into the 24-hour short story competitions in which I participate. I tried to think a little more outside the box for the contest.

She had always loved sports, especially football and golf. Golf was her favorite sport in which to participate while football was her favorite spectator sport. She had started watching football with her father from her earliest memories. Her favorite team was the Dallas Cowboys and as a young girl, she fantasized about becoming a Dallas Cowboys cheerleader, and marrying a quarterback. As a child, Nadine Miller got in fights whenever someone called her a tomboy. While she loved sports, she also loved wearing girly clothes, and dreaming of one day having a fairy tale wedding.

There was the time when Nadine was in third grade when she had gotten a new frilly pink dress for her best friend's birthday party. She had looked forward to Sally's party and thought she looked beautiful in her new party dress. Billy Andrews had teased her about being a 'tomboy in a pink dress'. She tried to ignore him at first, but when he wouldn't stop and a couple other boys joined in, Nadine tackled him to the ground, sitting on his chest and punching him in the face until Sally's father pulled her off.

Nadine's new dress was ruined; the lace was torn, there were grass stains all over, and the bodice was ripped. She cried all the way home. She had begged her father to buy the dress even though it had cost twice as much as he had told her she could spend on a party dress. She loved that dress, and she vowed never to talk to Billy Andrews again!

Billy's black eye was the talk of the school the next day. Their group class photograph, with Billy's black eye sticking out like a sore thumb, was proof through the years that nobody should call Nadine a tomboy. Billy never teased Nadine again.

The day after Sally's birthday party, Nadine's father had planned to golf with some buddies from work. Being a single father since his wife's death a few years earlier, Mr. Miller had arranged to leave Nadine with his late wife's parents for the day. However, Nadine was still so upset over the loss of her new party dress, he decided to take her for her first golf outing. She didn't play because that wouldn't be fair to the guys, but she enjoyed riding in the golf cart, and was interested in the game.

Nadine's father was so pleased that his beloved daughter showed such interest in his favorite pastime, that he took her shopping later that day for some golf clubs of her own. He then signed her up for her first golf lessons. She was a natural, and golfed often, and played on her high school golf team.

In her late twenties, Nadine started dating younger men. She was a cougar before she knew what a cougar was. She worked hard and she played hard. She often found that most men her age couldn't keep up with the energy she put into everything. She was more interested in being active, and doing outdoorsy things, than in the cocktail parties so many of her contemporaries were involved in. She enjoyed the occasional cocktail party, but golfing, hiking, biking, or watching football were her favorite activities away from work.

After college, Nadine became a real estate agent, and quickly rose to the top of her profession. Her work ethic and professionalism gained her tremendous respect among her clients and colleagues. She worked hard, and it paid off many times over. One Thursday afternoon, one of her colleagues invited her to a cocktail party that Saturday night. "I know you don't love parties, but there's a guy I really want you to meet. He's a mortgage broker, and he works hard and plays hard like you. If you don't like him, you can leave. I just want you to meet him. If nothing else, you might like his work ethic and work with him on some real estate transactions."

Against her better judgment, Nadine agreed to go to the party. After all, she had just purchased a new red cocktail dress that she just couldn't resist. The night of the party, Nadine went to her friend's condo and mingled. She was in the middle of a group of her co-workers who were teasing her about being a cougar. A stranger walked up just then and said, "Cougar in a red dress."

Nadine turned just as her friend walked up. "Oh, Nadine, I want you to meet Bill, William actually. William Andrews, I'd like you to meet Nadine Miller."

After nearly thirty years, Nadine and Billy were talking again. They found they had many of the same interests, the Dallas Cowboys, golfing, hiking, biking. They spent a lot of time with each other and soon became engaged.

Thirty years after that fateful birthday party at which Nadine's beautiful girly party dress had been ruined, she married Billy Andrews in a lovely, frilly, classy, and girly wedding dress. Just before getting into the limo to escape to their honeymoon, Nadine was ready to toss her bouquet to the vultures waiting to fight over the lovely floral morsel.

Dirty Laundry

Samantha Scott walked out of the dry cleaners. Placing her items in the back of her Explorer, she thought back to 1976 in Savannah, Georgia. It had been her job to iron her father's shirts for work. She used to cry about how much she hated him for making her iron his shirts in the middle of August when the heat was so terrible and she wanted to be swimming with her friends. She smiled now, thinking how her father had taught her good work ethic. There was always time for swimming when her chores were done, and the water felt all the better knowing she had done a great job and her Daddy would look great in court.

Alexander Scott had been the top criminal defense attorney in Savannah for decades. Her Daddy had followed in his Daddy's footsteps…and Samantha…she was a divorce lawyer. She just didn't have a mind for criminal law. She couldn't help but wish her Daddy was here now to help her with this case. Savannah was an excellent divorce attorney, almost always getting the best deal for her clients.

Things, however, had not gone in favor of Erica Crimson, a client she represented recently. The nasty divorce had been finalized a week before. Unfortunately, Howard Crimson was a powerful man in this county, and the judge had obviously been swayed politically. Erica had filed for divorce after finding Howard cheating on her for the third time. Since she had been a homemaker for years, raising their twins, she had asked for a sufficient maintenance until she could get on her feet. The amount they requested had been denied and she would only get a meager sum for six months, and she had to move out of the family home in a month. Erica and Howard had a loud argument on the courthouse steps following their bitter divorce proceedings.

Pulling away from the curb, Samantha thought about her conversation with Erica yesterday. Erica called her to ask her to represent her again. The thing was that Erica now needed an attorney to defend her because she had just been arrested for the murder of her ex-husband. "Erica, you know that I'm not a criminal attorney. You would be much better represented by a criminal attorney."

Erica shook her head, "No, Samantha, I want you to defend me!" She looked pleadingly at Samantha, "I know that you did everything you could have done for me in the divorce. It was only because of Howard's political ties that we didn't fare well. You're the only one who knows I'm not capable of killing anyone." Erica argued until Samantha gave in against her better judgment. Perhaps Erica should be the attorney.

The problem was that everyone had seen them arguing after court. Erica and Howard were both still living in the Crimson Mansion. They had bedrooms at opposite ends of the home, but nobody else was staying at the mansion. To top it all off, Erica didn't have an alibi. She said that she had taken some sleeping pills and had gone to bed early that night. Howard was found in his home office chair slumped over his desk, with a single gun shot wound in the back of his head. The murder weapon was lying on the floor next to him, wiped clean of prints.

"Oh, Daddy, what am I going to do? I don't even know where to start," Samantha said to her father, sitting next to his tombstone. She often came to the cemetery and spoke to her deceased father about her cases. "I'm really in over my head. I should never have agreed to defend Erica. I just couldn't tell her no even though that would have been the smart and kind thing to do. I botched her divorce case and I certainly don't want to botch her murder trial." Samantha started to cry. "Oh, Daddy, I just want to iron your shirts again. I can't do this!"

Suddenly Samantha remembered a case in which her father's client, a murder suspect, had no alibi, and her father had nothing to work with. He found that the only way to defend his client was to find the real killer. She knew that was her only chance, but the police had already investigated everyone. Howard had certainly had his share of enemies, but they had all been checked out. Where could she possibly look that the police already hadn't?

The police had checked out any possible enemies that Howard might have had. But did Erica have enemies? Did the police check that out? Highly unlikely. Erica had been the obvious suspect, and they didn't bother looking any further. Samantha remembered when Erica and Howard had married twenty years ago, Erica was pregnant. Howard had also been dating Claudia Brewer. Claudia and Erica were never friends, and it was likely that Howard was the reason for that. Claudia's husband had recently deserted her, leaving her penniless and living in an old trailer on the bad side of town.

Was it possible that Claudia killed Howard, knowing that Erica would likely be arrested? Had she really carried a grudge all these years?

The next morning, Samantha went to the diner where Claudia worked as a waitress, knowing there would be several cops having their coffee break. She sat at the booth next to them, knowing she had to get it right. When Claudia came over to take her order, Samantha said loudly, "I bet you're feeling good." Claudia looked at her quizzically, "Yes, I am feeling good today. How are you, Samantha?"

Samantha was silent, watching Claudia's eyes before she responded. She knew she had to get this right. "That's not exactly what I meant. I know you and Erica Crimson have never been friends; in fact, most would probably say you've been rivals. You wanted to marry Howard, didn't you?"

Claudia shrugged her shoulders, "Well, sure. Everyone knows I had my eyes on Howie in high school. So what?"

"You never forgave Erica for taking what you couldn't have. I think you were at the Crimson Mansion the night Howard was killed." Claudia fidgeted, looking like she was ready to take flight, and Samantha went on, "I think you tried to seduce Howard but he wouldn't have anything to do with you. After twenty years, you got your revenge on Erica by killing Howard, didn't you?"

Claudia lunged for Samantha's neck, "Why you little..."

Whitworth Essay

On the application to get into Whitworth College, there was an essay question. This is the question, and my answer. I believe there was a word count limit however I no longer remember what it was. After all, it was almost 20 years ago.

Describe a significant experience in your life and how it has shaped your definition of personal success.

Among the most significant experiences in my life, are my separation and divorce. While divorce is commonly viewed as a negative development, I look back on my divorce as a positive accomplishment.

I experienced a lot of personal growth during this time. I had to take over the roll of father as well as being a mother for my two sons. This brought many challenges my way. But it also helped me to realize what success really is. I hope to teach this to my children.

I used to think personal success was being wealthy. Now I know success has nothing to do with money. Personal success has to do with being happy and content within yourself; but not so much that you become stagnant. It means not settling for what you have, but continually setting goals and striving to reach them.

I was 28 years old when I wrote this…and now, at 47, I still believe it.

Tell No Lies

This story is actually the first chapter of my book, Rainbow in the Dark.

Brandi Demarco rushed home from the store with her groceries; baby Madison asleep in her car seat in back. Brandi wanted to get home and start cooking dinner before Rudy got home. He'd been so angry with her this morning, and she would do almost anything to keep from making him angry. Brandi worked part-time as a waitress and had gotten home later than usual because the car battery was dead when she tried to start her car after work. She worked the night shift in an all night diner so they wouldn't have to pay a sitter. The others leaving work at the same time had tried helping but since nobody had jumper cables, there was nothing to do but wait for her co-worker's husband to get there with his. She hadn't called Rudy since Jessica's husband was coming to pick her up anyway. This had caused her to get home almost an hour late.

Rudy had accused her of cheating on him, and slapped her across the face, which was minor compared to his treatment of her when he'd beat her recently. She told him what had happened, and he told her that he was going to check her story out, and that she better not be lying to him or she knew what would happen. Brandi did know what would happen as he had gotten progressively more violent and she wondered what happened to the gentle loving boy she met in her freshman year in college.

Rudy had been so caring, completely doting on her all the time. He had always been the epitome of a gentleman, opening doors for her, carrying her books, holding her coat for her to put it on. They had met in their first class the first day of the school year at Central Washington University. They had fallen in love with each other quickly and were often together both in and out of school. They had similar goals and wanted to be teachers, so they were lucky enough to have several classes together the first year.

A few months into their second year of college Brandi found out she was pregnant. She was against abortion, so that had not been an option. Rudy had proposed to Brandi the weekend after they found out she was pregnant and suggested a wedding the next summer, and she had thought that to be a very gallant gesture. A month after spring quarter ended the two had married, and Madison Rose was born a month after that. Rudy had been attentive to her throughout the pregnancy, attending to all her needs. After Madison was born, he continued to be a model husband for the first couple of months. Everything changed after that.

Initially it seemed like a gradual change, and at first it was just that Rudy didn't do as much for her. Brandi was actually more comfortable with that anyway. She thought he had gone overboard in doing things for her. Soon after that change, Rudy started getting more domineering, telling her when and how to take care of Madison, and the house, and constantly inquiring as to what she had done, who she had seen each day. Brandi thought he might be stressed about finances, and she thought it was time for her to find a job anyway. When she suggested it to him, she thought he would appreciate the fact that she was thinking of him and their futures, but instead he reacted badly to it. He accused her of wanting to get away from him.

He was also acting jealous of the baby, accusing her of loving the baby more than him, and Brandi had taken to leaving Madison in her crib most of the time when Rudy was home because she was afraid of the baby getting hurt. He had gotten very physical with her and she had actually ended up in the hospital after the beatings two times in as many months. She never would have thought Rudy would do these things, but now she had to think of Madison. This was not what she wanted for her daughter.

Brandi's parents had noticed a difference in her during their phone calls. They had mentioned it several times, but she made light of it every time she talked to them. She just knew Rudy was just going through a temporary change and when the stress eased up things would go back to normal. She just knew that she needed to work harder to not upset him. She didn't want to let on that anything was wrong because her parents had always liked Rudy and she didn't want their opinion of him to be affected. They were planning to visit in just 3 weeks and Brandi hoped and prayed Rudy would overcome whatever had been making her once gentle husband so violent before they arrived in Ellensburg.

After pulling up to the little cottage they rented from Brandi's grandfather, she carried Madison into the house and put her in the crib. She brought the groceries in and started dinner; spaghetti and garlic bread with salad. She made sure to plan something that Rudy would like, but was neither too expensive nor too cheap. She had to be so careful lately trying to calculate how Rudy would react to everything and plan her actions accordingly. Fortunately Brandi always used her mother-in-law's spaghetti recipe so Rudy was always pleased when she made it. She hoped this would put him in a better mood. She was terrified it wouldn't.

The sauce was simmering on the stove, the garlic bread had just been put in the oven and the noodles were nearly done to al dente the way he liked them, when she heard the sound of Rudy's motorcycle outside. Her heart immediately started pounding nearly out of her chest. She had been dreading Rudy's return home all day, and she needed to get control of herself; she felt like she might hyperventilate. Taking the lettuce and other vegetables from the refrigerator, Brandi took some deep cleansing breaths before starting to prepare the salad. She concentrated on slowing her breathing, and chopped the lettuce. Rudy walked in and Brandi turned to look at him, hoping to read his mood by studying his face.

"Hi sweetie, how was your day?" she asked him.

He looked at her and then around the room without responding. Brandi could tell he was thinking about things that had gone on between them that morning so felt she should do something to take his mind off that and onto better things. Otherwise he might fly into a rage over something that was beyond her control, and in which he was fabricating things in his mind. She had become increasingly afraid of the man who she had thought was so tender and kind.

"Rudy, I was thinking how nice it would be if your parents could come for a visit soon. Do you think they could get away? They haven't been able to see Madison yet."

He looked at her, again without responding. She couldn't read his face. It was almost as if he had become someone else. All of a sudden he said, "Did you forget what you did this morning?" He grabbed her wrist roughly.

"Rudy, you're hurting me! I told you the battery was dead in the car when I got off work. Did you ask around? Everyone at work can verify it."

He released her and said, "I don't need to ask around. I already know you're lying to me! You're not going back to work. I called your boss and told him that you wouldn't be back. I want you at home so I know where you are. I don't want some other man worming his way into your pants."

"Rudy, what are you talking about? There is no other man. You know that I love you. I'm only interested in you. I have never cheated on you and I never will!"

"Then tell no lies!"

Rudy watched her face, saying nothing. He walked out of the room and Brandi realized she had been holding her breath. She knew he had left the room to take his shoes off and to inspect the house; looking for anything out of place. It's not that he thought she wasn't keeping the house clean. It was that he was looking for evidence that she was untrustworthy.

Brandi hated this feeling of fear that she had developed toward her husband. When she had been in the hospital after he had hit her hard enough to rupture her kidney, a victim advocate from the local domestic violence shelter had come in and talked to her about the cycles of violence. Brandi had denied any abuse claiming that she had fallen from the neighbor's horse. She had listened intently because she knew what the lady was saying was accurate. Rudy had bought her flowers or cards after he beat her in the beginning and he always said he was sorry and promised it would never happen again. He didn't even do that any more. If she just would have had the coffee ready when he got up, he wouldn't have had to hit her. If she would have washed the shirt he wanted to wear, she wouldn't have gotten beaten. If she wouldn't have been talking on the phone when he got home, he wouldn't have had to punch her. He always blamed her for the beatings. She was seriously considering the advice that had been given to her that day in the hospital. She still wished things would just go back to the way they were, but as things kept getting progressively worse she was losing any hope of that happening.

Brandi kept her mind on making the salad and having it ready when he came back to the kitchen. She finished the salad and put it on the table, which she had set before starting dinner. She drained the noodles, took the bread from the oven and poured the sauce into a bowl. She put all of that on the table and started to tidy the kitchen when Rudy walked back in.

"Dinner's on the table, sweetheart," she told him. He whipped around, slapping her across the face just as he had that morning when she came home. Her hand reached up to her cheek.

"Don't think I don't know what you're doing! You're making my mother's spaghetti because you feel guilty for cheating and you think I'm stupid," Rudy said, punching her in the stomach.

As Brandi doubled over, Rudy grabbed her by the hair, pulling her face up to his to his, "You're so predictable!" He shoved her, slamming her into the kitchen counter. Brandi closed her eyes at she connected with the counter and pain shot through her body. Rudy punched her in the lower back, and Brandi felt the same pain as when he had injured her kidney. Madison started to cry. Brandi's eyes shot open, and she saw the knife on the counter that she had been using to chop the vegetables for the salad. Without thinking, she grabbed the knife, swinging around, trying to protect herself. Rudy was caught unaware and the knife sliced his throat as Brandi closed her eyes and swung high and wide.

Brandi opened her eyes to see Rudy had fallen to the floor, with blood spurting from his neck. She had severed the carotid artery. Rudy was already weak from blood loss, and looked at her, "What have you done to me bitch?"

The baby was crying loudly and Brandi screamed. She looked at Rudy, and ran to get towels. She came back with towels and started to apply pressure just as he slumped, his eyes vacant. Rudy was dead.

The Birthday Gift

Brenda watched her son as he tied his shoes. He was going to the movie with his friend and his family at the mall's cinema. When he returned, and Brenda's husband got home from work, they would go out to dinner to celebrate Brenda's birthday. Brenda had been healing emotionally from her third miscarriage. She had not been handling things well but found a great therapist and was finally getting back to normal.

"Are you ready, Bobby?"

Her son nodded, "Yes, Mommy."

She gave him a hug. "I know that I have not been a good mommy lately. I have been so sad that I was having a hard time showing you my love. But I promise I will do better now."

"Don't worry, Mommy. I know. The baby died. I was sad too," he told her in a tone far more mature than his age. He suddenly brightened and said, "Mommy, I'm going to bring you home a birthday present."

Brenda smiled, "Oh, sweetie, you are my birthday present." She felt life's circumstances had forced him to grow up in some ways and that made her feel guilty because of her reaction to the miscarriage. They heard a knock at the door and Brenda said, "You enjoy the movie and we will go to dinner after you and Daddy are both home."

After closing the door, Brenda heard the dryer buzz to signal the cycle was done. She turned on the radio and folded the towels that were in the dryer. After putting the towels away, she sat down to check her email. She hadn't even turned her computer on in a couple of days, so her email inbox was flooded, especially with birthday wishes.

Brenda had been reading her email for nearly half an hour, when an Amber alert came over the radio. Her heart instantly started thumping harder. She flew across the room to turn the volume up. A baby had been abducted just minutes before. It was taken from it's stroller in the middle of a store in the mall. She breathed easier knowing that she didn't have to worry about Bobby and that the Amber alert was not for anyone she knew, but felt so sad for the parents and concerned for the baby.

Still getting over her last miscarriage, Brenda was especially emotional, and started to cry, and wished she was not alone. She knew how hard it was to lose a baby while still pregnant. All three of her miscarriages had occurred in her first trimester when she had just gotten used to the idea that she was going to have a baby. She could only imagine the pain of having a baby you have already bonded with disappearing and the anguish the parents must be feeling not knowing whether their baby would be found.

Brenda tried calling her husband but got his voice mail. He should be on his way home from work by now. She turned on the television hoping to get more information. There was a news bulletin about the abduction. It seems the parents had been looking at baby items inside the Baby Gap store. They had not seen anyone come in, nor had any of the store clerks. According to the news report, security was in the process of looking at the security videos, but so far had seen nothing.

The phone rang, startling Brenda and causing her to jump. She grabbed the phone, "James?"

"No, Brenda, it's Sandy." Sandy was the mother of Bobby's friend, who he had gone to the movie with. "I can't find Bobby. He had to go to the bathroom, so I walked out to the lobby with him, and after waiting for quite a long time, I asked one of the theatre employees to check on him. He wasn't in there. I went back to the seat, but he hadn't gone back there. I don't know how he could have gotten past me. I was standing right next to the bathroom. I should have had Paul take him to that bathroom. Brenda, I'm so sorry! We'll find him. I just wanted to let you know what's going on."

"Sandy, a baby was abducted from the mall. There was an Amber Alert just a little while ago!" Brenda felt like she was going to collapse. "Oh my God, my Bobby!"

"Brenda, I'll be right there. Paul will keep looking and we've called the police. I'm sure they'll be notifying you soon."

"No, Brenda, just stay there to look for him. I'll be there as soon as James gets home. Where could Bobby have gone? I just can't..." The kitchen door opened, just and Bobby came in carrying a bundle hugged tightly to him.

"Happy Birthday, Mommy!!"

The Hitchhiker

I did something really stupid, with no regard for my safety. I picked up a hitchhiker. I *never* pick up hitchhikers! On this particular day, I was feeling bored and lonely, and still had a long drive ahead of me. I had left Atlanta, Georgia a few days before. I woke up that morning in Butte, Montana, and since I would be driving to Portland, Oregon that day, another long day of driving alone was before me.

The company I work for had offered me a huge promotion, along with an attractive raise in pay, which involved relocating from Atlanta to Portland. I was excited to move to a different part of the country, and to a fresh start. I opted to drive rather than having my car shipped to me. I had been excited to see the country from the driver's seat. I had truly enjoyed my solitude until this final day of my road trip. I was starting to get bored with my own company and wasn't looking forward to another day alone with my thoughts.

I ate breakfast at Denny's and was headed toward the freeway, just about to drive onto the on ramp when I spotted a man holding a sign which read, "Going to Spokane? I'll buy the gas." He was clean cut and looked harmless. He was an attractive man around my age, about six feet tall, with dark hair and a slender build. If I had longer to think about it, I might have talked myself out of stopping. As it was, I had only a split second, and instantly pulled to a stop next to him. Pressing the button to roll down the passenger window, I told him I could take him to Spokane. He smiled and thanked me as he opened the door and got in my car.

"Thanks for the ride! I'm Matt. My buddy, Joe, was supposed to meet me in Butte this weekend so we could ride to Spokane together," he said in explanation of why he needed a ride.

"Nice to meet you, Matt. I'm Jessica. I'm on my way to Portland, so Spokane is right on my way." I looked over at Matt, and felt like my initial assessment of him had been accurate. He had a boy-next-door quality, and I felt comfortable with him. We chatted easily, and he explained that he lived in Spokane and had come to Butte with his cousin for a wedding. His friend was supposed to also come to the wedding and had been visiting relatives near Casper, Wyoming the week before. His cousin was headed to Minnesota after the wedding, so Matt's plan had been to ride back to Spokane with Joe. Unfortunately, Joe's grandfather had a heart attack the day before he was to leave for the wedding. "My first thought was to rent a car and drive back to Spokane. I thought I would take the more adventurous solution and hitchhike. I figured that would be a great way to meet people I otherwise wouldn't have," Matt further explained.

I told Matt about my job promotion and relocation to Portland. I told him about my job, and he told me about his job. We talked about our families and it soon seemed like we had known each other far longer than just a couple of hours. The time was definitely going faster than it would have if I had driven past Matt that morning.

When we were nearing Kellogg, Idaho, I decided I needed to stretch my legs. Matt suggested we find a gas station, and he would fill up the tank. While Matt was gassing up my car, I went inside to use the restroom. I decided to pick up some snacks and something to drink. As I was approaching the check out counter, I noticed the television with a news program on. There was a breaking news story. The story was about a man who they believed to have murdered two women and attempted to kill another woman when each of them picked him up hitchhiking. I felt an instant feeling of dread, and my mind was racing. I had to make sure Matt did not get back in my car,

While it was true that I didn't know that Matt was the same man, it just didn't feel right to let him back into my car. Just then, the television station showed a composite sketch of the suspect. He looked just like Matt. The news anchor reported that the woman who escaped from this man told police that she had picked up the hitchhiker, who had seemed so normal, so clean cut and safe. Oh my God, that was my first impression of Matt. She said that they had talked in the car, and the hitchhiker, who had told her his name was Max, was very personable and offered to pay for gas. They had pulled off the road into a gas station, and "Max" pumped the gas while she went inside to use the restroom. After Max bought each of them a coffee, he offered to drive. He turned onto a dirt road and stopped the car in a thicket of trees. Just as she asked what he was doing, the hitchhiker pulled a short rope out of his jacket pocket. She told police that she had thrown her hot coffee in his face and jumped out of the car, running as fast as she could until someone else came along. Police had found her car with no sign of "Max".

There was no way that I was going to let Matt, or whatever his name was, back into my car. I paid for my items, and realized Matt was inside. I had no idea how long he had been standing there. I decided the best thing to do would be to tell him he could no longer ride with me while I was still inside where there were others around. He came nearer and my heart raced. I knew that I just needed to tell him he was on his own while I was still at the counter. Hopefully the people working would recognize him from the news, and report him. Once I was in my car and away from him, I would call 9-1-1.

"Matt, you will have to get to Spokane on your own. I have changed my mind about giving you a ride."

"I saw the news report, Jessica. I understand how you feel. I saw that sketch and if I didn't know better, I would have thought that guy was me too. I can assure you that I am not the killer, but I understand how you feel. Thank you for getting me this far." He turned to walk out the door.

That was too easy. I thought he might get violent. I needed to hurry out to my car and get away from there as quickly as I could. I shouted, "Call the police! It's the hitchhiking killer." And with that, I ran to my car, fearing that Matt would turn around and come back. I could see that Matt had gotten across the street. It seemed he wasn't coming back this way, and I relaxed a little since I could see him walking away from me.

As I reached for my car door I heard from behind me, "Can I get a ride, ma'am?" I froze. I could still see Matt walking away. I started to turn and the man said, "I just need a ride to Coeur d'Alene. I'll be happy to give you money for gas."

"No! I will not give you a ride," I shouted. "Get away from me."

"Calm down, lady. I just asked for a ride."

"I will not calm down. Go away!" The man grabbed my arm and reached for my door handle, which I had unlocked as I had walked close to my car. He was pushing me inside. As I started to scream, he held his hand over my mouth. Was this Max? I only got a glimpse of him, but from what I could see, he looked like the sketch I had seen on the news. I was so terrified I couldn't even think about how to get away. Why had I been so stupid? Was my poor decision going to cost me my life? I needed to pull myself out of this and fight.

Suddenly, I heard something behind "Max" and he slumped to the ground. Looking out, I saw Max lying on the ground with a large rock next to him. I saw Matt standing there, and heard sirens. Matt had saved me and the police were on their way. I was safe!

Melanie Young

Car Trouble

This is something I wrote in English Composition 101 in college, in Maury Barr's class. We all loved Maury! I am not changing anything from the original paper I wrote back in 1991. Read on...you'll read about one of my biggest fears coming true...

Cars, in general, are a big problem. Sometimes, automobiles are far more trouble than they're worth. For one thing, cars are a major expense: the cost of the car itself, insurance, gas, maintenance. The list goes on and on.

Some makes and models seem more prone to mechanical defects and breakdowns than others. A brand new car might be continually in the shop for one problem after another. This can test your patience, and your warranty. On the other hand, you may have an older vehicle and never have any problems or breakdowns.

Owning a vehicle is more of a necessity than a luxury in our society, especially in rural areas. Between chauffeuring kids around, grocery shopping, going to work or school, and getting to all the appointments and commitments we always seem to have, it's almost impossible to get by without a car. In fact, when fate leaves us without a vehicle, it can disrupt our lives entirely.

Recently, my car broke down. At a most inopportune moment, my trusty chariot failed me; I was in the drive-thru at McDonald's. The clutch just ceased functioning. Oh no! One of my worst nightmares had come true! The car is eleven years old and hasn't caused me any inconvenience since I've owned it, until now! With a foot of snow on the ground, and a temperature of thirty degrees, was grateful that my young sons were not with me.

One of the managers helped me push my car out of the drive-thru and said I could leave it there until I could get some help. Now I had fifteen minutes to make it to my first day of college English Composition class. I made it there with only minutes to spare and managed to devour most of my Quarter Pounder before class started.

It was not easy to keep my mind off my car concerns and on the class. I knew my older son, who was supposed to walk to the college when he got out of school would go home instead if he saw that my car was not in the college parking lot. He would be locked out of the apartment alone for a least a half-hour in the cold. So when we had a break, I ran to the phone to call my son's school. I also called my mother, who was taking care of my younger son, who had the chicken pox. With those tasks out of the way, I could go back to worrying about my car.

What was wrong with my car? Would it cost more than it was worth to repair it? As a single mother, my income was very limited. Needless to say, I was overwhelmed!

My major concern, for the moment, was getting my car home. I knew it would have to wait for my father or my brother, Ron, to retrieve it for me. After classes were out for the day, and my children and I were safely home, there was nothing I could do but wait. I have a strong aversion to waiting!!

After a two hour wait, Ron finally came. He managed to tow my car to my apartment, and he checked it out there. Now for the bad news. I was nervously anticipating hearing that there was something gravely wrong with my poor little green Toyota.

It turned out that the master cylinder on my clutch was no good. Well, being so mechanically minded as I am, that meant absolutely nothing to me. I asked Ron to explain to me exactly what that meant, and of course, it all went right over my head. I remembered the two most important points: what part to ask for, and the approximate price.

The first thing I did was to call the wrecking yard to check on used parts. I don't know why I bothered. Every time I call the local auto graveyard, they tell me they had the part I need, but they had just sold it. Déjà vu. It happened again!

Next, I called one of the car parts stores in town and surprisingly, the cylinder was in stock and would cost a few dollars less than Ron had guessed it would. I bought the part and waited. I waited for my father to have time to repair the "Green Machine." I waited for two more days.

Finally, my dad had time to work on the car. Now we moved my Corolla to my parents' house, where it would be more convenient for my father to work on it. And again, I waited. However, I thought I was waiting for the last time. Ron came over to help my father with the repairs. They seemed to be taking an awfully long time. At last, they came in the house. It didn't look good. They needed another part. The slave cylinder was also leaking and would have to be replaced. That doesn't sound so bad, except it was Sunday afternoon – in Colville, Washington. There were no parts stores open. Then my dad remembered an auto parts store in nearby Kettle Falls that was open on Sundays. He called them, only to discover they were out of stock.

We would have to wait until Monday to get the part. So I waited. And I went another day without transportation. I was starting to feel like I was in the Twilight Zone every time I needed to go somewhere.

Monday came and I begged rides to school, the store, and to my parents' house. By this time, I was beginning to think I would never get my car back on the road again. Dad came home from work and I felt guilty that he would be working on my car instead of relaxing and eating his dinner. Still, I was tired of waiting. So I sent my father out into the cold while I sat in the house, waiting beside the crackling fire.

After five long days, I wasn't sure I believed it when Dad said he was finished. For a few days I treated my car like a baby, afraid that something would go wrong. But now that all seems to be going well, I've gone back to darting around town in my "Green Machine"…believing in its reliability once again.

Regretfully, I sound ungrateful in this essay for all the work my father, and also my brother put in to help me. I was grateful, but my concern at the time I wrote this was that I should do well on the essay and get a good grade. I'm proud to say that I scored a 4.0 on this paper. I think Maury was generous!

The Witness

Ellen didn't take the time to pull any boots on her feet before she ran out the garden door into the snow. The man she had seen kill the gas station attendant the day before was trying to get in the back door.

She hadn't been able to sleep because every time she closed her eyes she saw the poor young man being shot in the chest over and over. Ellen had just finished pumping her gas and was getting back into her car when she looked up to see the clerk right before the robber shot him. She slammed her door shut and fumbled with her key for a few seconds before she was able to get her car started and sped away. She called in an anonymous tip to the police that evening and spent a sleepless night reliving the horrifying event.

Ellen told nobody at work the next day about witnessing the shooting, although it was the talk of the office because shootings were so rare in the quiet little town. She left work early in the afternoon claiming she had a headache. She was afraid of being identified as the witness to the shooting. The thought of the killer coming after her never left her mind.

Once Ellen arrived home, she decided her plan to come home had been a bad one. She felt safer being around people. She locked everything up tight. She tried to occupy herself doing some laundry hoping to take her mind off the young man dropping to the floor in the gas station.

She took the towels from the dryer and walked into the living room, noticing the snow had started to fall as she passed by the picture window. Ellen turned the TV on to occupy her mind while she folded the towels, realizing instantly what a mistake it was because the fatal shooting at the gas station the day before was headline news. She quickly turned it back off but wondered if she should have watched. Maybe she would hear that they'd arrested the killer and she could relax.

Carrying the basket of towels up the stairs, Ellen started to formulate a plan to go to the police station in the morning. She had initially wanted to be anonymous thinking if the police didn't know who she was the killer wouldn't either. But now she was thinking she might be able to rely on a little protection if she told the police who she was. She was just finishing putting the towels away in the bathroom when she heard a car door close. It sounded like it came from the alley, and she looked out the bathroom window and saw an older model pickup in the alley and someone dressed in black trudging through the snow toward her back door.

Ellen quietly came down the stairs and as she reached the bottom, she could hear someone at the back door. She wrapped her robe tighter around her and slipped out the side door. She walked through the garden, turning to look back at her house every few steps. She obviously hadn't taken the time to think before coming out the door. With only slippers on her feet, her toes were already frozen. She should have grabbed her cell phone before leaving her house.

As she went through the gate, Ellen thought she heard the storm door on her house slam shut. She turned her head and looked back, she saw the person in black coming towards her. She started to cry as she pushed on through the snow, running over the train tracks. The snow was falling so heavily, she was finding it difficult to see very far in front of her. She turned to see where the person who was chasing her was, and couldn't see anything through the falling snow. Turning back to try to see where she was going, she saw a bright light out of the corner of her eye. She heard a train whistle, turned again and then saw in the light the killer's face she had seen the day before, just a split second before the train slammed into him.

Lesser of Two Evils

April was excited to move into her new home. It was an adorable little house across the road from the lake. She had chosen this one because it made her think of a story book cottage. It was so warm and cozy. She knew she would always feel safe and comfortable in this home. It was a quiet neighborhood, and the view of the lake from her house was amazing.

When April came to look at the house with her real estate agent, she knew immediately this was the house she wanted to buy. She still asked him to bring her back to it two more times before she made her decision. She wanted to see the home and neighborhood at different times of the day to make sure she still had a good feeling about it after dark. Being a single woman, she figured she couldn't be too careful.

The house was a craftsman style white brick cottage with red trimmed windows and a red front door. The yard was completely fenced and there was a lovely rose garden in the back. The entire yard was impeccably landscaped with a great variety of flowers, trees and shrubbery. It was pleasing to the eye no matter where you looked and wasn't overdone. Next to the rose garden was a rock patio and she couldn't wait to sit and enjoy her morning coffee on her patio. The house was on the small side, but all she needed. There were two bedrooms, as well as a cozy room for her to use as an office and library. The bright and cheery kitchen was wonderful, with a window looking out at her new rose garden. The blue granite countertops were gorgeous; the ivory ceramic tile floor and the ivory cabinets were a perfect compliment to the counters. The home couldn't be more suited to April if she had picked everything out herself.

Arriving before the movers, April parked on the street and went into the house for a walk through to make sure the placement she had in mind for the furniture was really what she wanted. Walking through her new home, she knew that her furnishings would be perfect in the spots she had chosen to place them and was excited for the movers to get there so she could truly make this her home. April opened up the house and waited patiently for the movers to get there. It was a fabulous morning. The sun was shining, glistening off the lake across the street from her home. The birds were singing in a joyous serenade. The gentle breeze was rustling through the rose bushes and pine trees, creating a wonderful assault of pleasant aromas.

April was lost in her appreciation of the morning and her new environment when the movers pulled up to her house. She snapped out of it and walked quickly to the truck to greet them. "Good morning," she called to them as they got out of the truck, with *Al B. Movin'* painted on the side. There were three men there to unload the truck.

The driver, Al Bates, walked over and shook her hand, "Good morning, ma'am. Won't take long to unload. Tell us where you want things and stay out of the way." He was abrupt but actually sounded polite.

April smiled, "I know right where I want all the furniture and the boxes are all clearly marked – I have written the room where I want them on top of each box."

He gave her a nod, and the men went to work unloading the truck. It didn't take long, just as Al had promised. They were nearly finished when she noticed one of the men admiring one of her paintings which she had unwrapped. "Do you collect art?" April asked him.

"No ma'am, I just noticed this one and thought it looked real nice."

"Yes, well, my paintings are the only thing I splurge on. With everything else, I'm a bargain shopper," she told him, smiling as she said it. "I really enjoy fine art."

"Is this worth a lot?"

April was a little taken aback by this question, considering it rude to ask about the value of another person's belongings, but decided the man was just uncultured and seemed more interested than rude, "Well, like I said, I tend to splurge on the paintings I buy. This is my most valuable one."

The men placed all the furniture where she wanted and left April to her unpacking. She unpacked all the kitchen boxes and put everything in the cupboards and moved on to the bathrooms, followed by her bedroom and then the office. She didn't have many boxes, so the unpacking went quickly. When she was done, she poured herself a glass of Pinot Noir and walked out onto the patio and relaxed in the afternoon shade. She knew she would be happy here for many years.

April came home from work on Tuesday feeling happy. Her boss had told her she was receiving a raise unexpectedly and she was floating on air. She had been living in her home on the lake for just over two weeks and felt that life just couldn't get any better. It was late spring and the sun was shining brilliantly still; she would be able to enjoy her dinner on the patio.

Parking her car in the garage, April noticed a car parked across the street by the lake. There was a wide spot there, and she figured there would be people parking there a lot to enjoy the gorgeous view. She closed the garage door, and locked her car before going into the house.

After looking through her mail, April made a salad for dinner and poured herself a glass of Chardonnay. She turned on the radio just loud enough to be able to hear it through the patio door and walked out onto the patio with her dinner. It was a beautiful evening and she could tell by their singing that the birds were just as happy as she was to have this glorious day to enjoy. She ate her dinner and relaxed while she finished her wine and when she went into the house it was still a little light out but starting to get dark.

April put her dishes into the dishwasher and walked over to the living room window, noticing the car she had seen earlier was still parked there. It was too cold to be swimming but knowing nothing about fishing, wondered if that was what the car's owner was doing. Just before she turned away, she noticed someone was sitting in the car.

A week had gone by and April noticed the same dark blue car parked by the lake each evening when she came home from work. She felt a little uncomfortable since she had noticed someone sitting in the car every time she took the time to look close enough. April silently chided herself for letting her imagination spook her. Still when she came home the next evening and saw the same car sitting there with someone in it, she decided to walk across the street and talk to the person in the car, just to make herself feel better. As she neared the car it started up and the driver pulled away.

Upon returning home from work the following evening the car was not parked there and April thought she had probably been right about the person fishing and it had just been a coincidence that the driver had been in the car when she took the time to notice whether anyone was there. Perhaps fishing season was over and there was no longer any reason for the blue car to be parked across from her house. Feeling more confident, April walked into her house just as her phone started to ring. It was her brother, Mark, who was coming for a visit the next weekend with his wife. April and Mark chatted for several minutes, and as she had a tendency to do when she was talking on the phone April walked around her house. At one point she walked past the living room window and saw the dark blue car parked across the street; there was someone sitting in the driver's seat. When she mentioned it to Mark and explained how the same car had been there almost every day for the past couple of weeks, Mark told her to hang up and call the police.

April called the police and told the officer on the phone about the car being parked across the street so often. She was told that since it is public property there is no crime in parking next to the lake but that they would have a patrol car drive by. It was only about ten minutes later that she saw a police car drive by and she felt more secure. A little while later she heard a knock on the door. She opened it to see a police officer standing there. He told her that he had talked to the man in the blue car who had explained that he had been sketching the lake and had even shown the officer some of his sketches. "They weren't very good, but I'm no art critic," the officer joked. He told her that the man had said he wouldn't be parking there anymore. He also reassured her that he would drive by while on patrol in the evenings

A week went by and true to his word the man in the dark blue car never came back. April had a wonderful visit with her brother and sister-in-law that weekend, which was Memorial Day Weekend, and they had even picnicked and gone swimming in the lake across from April's home. The visit went by much too quickly and Monday evening Mark and his wife left to drive back to their home in the city. April was feeling lonely after having guests all weekend and started to pace out of boredom and loneliness. She went to the living room window and saw a black car parked across the street by the lake. Although it wasn't the same car, April had a bad feeling about it. She checked all her locks and decided to put in a movie to lighten her mood. She didn't know why she was being so silly about this. She chose a comedy, put it in her DVD player and relaxed on the sofa, forgetting about her worries.

A strange noise startled April awake and she realized she had fallen asleep watching the movie. The same tune was playing over and over as DVD's often do when the movie has been over for some time. She wondered what the noise was that had awakened her, but instantly had the feeling that someone was in her house. She wanted to call the police but was frozen with fear. She remembered that she had forgotten her cell phone in her car. She had a phone in her bedroom and one in her office at opposite ends of the house. She tried to figure out where the sound had come from to decide which phone to go to. Since she had actually been asleep when she heard the sound, she didn't even know for sure that there had been anything at all. Perhaps it had been the DVD making the noise.

April gave herself a silent lecture and then went to her bedroom to get the phone. She thought she would get the phone and dial while she looked around the house. She remembered that she had double checked all the locks before she had fallen asleep. The police were going to think she was a paranoid kook. She picked up the phone just as a hand covered her mouth and an arm came around the other side of her body pinning her arms at her side. She tried to struggle and the phone dropped to the floor.

All of a sudden, she was shoved to the ground and her attacker was immediately on top of her. He backhanded her across the face and she screamed out in pain and terror. He ripped open April's blouse as she tried to grab his arms to stop him. She felt another blow to the other side of her face and screamed again. Never before had she felt such fear. She didn't know whether he intended to rape her or kill her...or both. She just knew that she had to fight back. From somewhere deep inside her, April suddenly felt an adrenaline rush and started wildly swinging her arms, trying to hit him and that's when he punched her hard in the stomach and then put his hands to her throat and starting choking her.

April was trying to scream but with her assailant's hands wrapped firmly around her throat she couldn't get any sound out. It didn't take long before everything started to go black. Suddenly the man fell to one side and was lying unconscious partially on top of her. April was in a fog and couldn't understand what had happened but instinct told her to flee and she started struggling to get out from under him.

She realized that there was someone else there moving the man off her. She looked up and the man she saw looked like the man who had been parking across the road. She suddenly recognized him as the mover who had admired her painting. She screamed and started scooting away. "Don't be frightened. I won't hurt you. We better get out of here because I don't know if this guy is going to come around," the mysterious man told her. She saw a single daisy on the floor.

He helped her up and grabbed her bedspread off the bed to wrap around her and they started out of the room as the man on the floor came around and grabbed April's ankle. There was a knock at the door, but none of them noticed as the mover stomped on the other man's arm to make him release April's ankle. The front door burst open and a couple of police officers appeared. April fainted.

April came around and found that she was on a gurney being loaded into an ambulance. One of the police officers noticed she was awake and came over to talk to her, "You're very lucky that this man was parked across from your house, young lady," he said, indicating the man standing next to the police car. "We believe the man who broke into your house and assaulted you tonight is the serial killer known as 'The Daisy Strangler.' He has murdered at least twelve women, after raping them, and leaves a daisy across their stomach. We found a daisy on the floor of your bedroom. The man who called us tonight said he was parked across the street and saw the killer break into your house. He went in to help you after calling us and he probably saved your life. He also admitted that he was planning to break into your house to steal a painting. Unfortunately, we can't arrest him for intent to steal." He looked at the mover, and then back to April, "It seems he is the lesser of two evils."

MY M.S.

I wrote this in 2002 shortly after being diagnosed with Multiple Sclerosis. Writing this 'essay' was basically just therapeutic at the time. I don't think I had any other purpose for writing it. It's obvious there is some bitterness. The reason I decided to include this in my book is because while Multiple Sclerosis is different for every person who has this disease, some people may share some of the feelings I had during this time. If this can help someone understand what somebody they care about is going through, or help someone validate their own feelings, then there is a purpose for my having written it. Keep in mind that some people with MS might share none of my emotions.

What is Multiple Sclerosis? Multiple Sclerosis is a chronic neurological disease that affects the nervous system. It is one of many autoimmune diseases. Because it affects the brain, it can affect every human function. The cause is unknown and there is no cure. That is as scientific as this is going to get.

When you are first diagnosed with multiple sclerosis, you have to go through the stages. There seems to be an unwritten rule about that. It doesn't matter how intelligent, experienced, or educated you are; you *have* to go through the stages. The stages are similar to mourning. The first is denial. There are different degrees of denial; ranging from wishing it was something else, to "there is no way that MS is what is wrong with me..." Some people have had symptoms for years without knowing what was wrong, and even wondering if there really was something wrong other than them going crazy since there sometimes seems to be no reason for the symptoms, that they welcome a diagnosis; so for them the denial may be short-lived and minor. For me, my denial was so strong that I yelled at my neurologist on the phone when he called me at 7:00 pm to talk to me about coming into the office to discuss treatment, and I told him I didn't need to go on treatment because there was nothing wrong with me; all my symptoms were getting better and they had been caused by something else. Hello, stupid! (Speaking to myself here.) That's what relapsing remitting MS does. When you have a relapse, exacerbation, attack, whatever you choose to call it, it gets better (remission) and your symptoms go away or get better after a few days, or a few weeks. My denial lasted a while; I researched other diseases trying to *make* myself have something else, anything else.

The research seems to be a requirement also. I don't know an MS patient who hasn't researched the disease, at least when first diagnosed, almost to obsession. Most are like me, and continue to research, and follow all the current studies, and the research goes on. You just have to find a happy medium so that you don't get overwhelmed, which is easy to do. It's so important to have a balance. Depression tends to be a problem with those with multiple sclerosis (in fact, it is one of the common symptoms), and getting too involved in research, at least for me, can lead to depression.

For me, the second stage was anger and depression, combined (which are closely related emotions anyway). Some days I was just depressed all day. I couldn't seem to pull myself out of it. Other days, I could be so angry one minute that I didn't want anyone talking to me, or being happy around me, and then the next minute I was so depressed I would be crying and acting like a pathetic, pessimistic, self-absorbed neuropath. Yet, whenever my neurologist asked if I was suffering from depression, I firmly denied any depression. I held up a strong front. That's something that didn't change about me; I have always been the type to try to make sure people knew as little as possible about anything wrong with me. I still struggle with depression at times. Some days, I have a hard time not getting weepy about little things.

Multiple Sclerosis is different for everyone. You could ask 100 MS patients what MS is and you would get 100 different answers. There are some of the more common symptoms that the majority of MS patients have – like fatigue, and less common symptoms that only a few have – hearing loss for instance. Some days my body hurts so badly and is so stiff, I just want to go soak in a Jacuzzi; today is one of those days. That is referred to as spasticity. I don't know who names some of these things. When I hear spasticity, I think of something like seizures. That is not what spasticity is. It has to do with the muscles having spasms that you don't even see, but they cause pain and stiffness in the muscles. My worst symptoms currently include hearing loss, blind spots in one eye, memory problems, fatigue, sleep problems, spasticity, and urinary frequency and urgency.

It's not unusual for individuals with MS to refer to "my MS." 'That's not my MS' you might hear someone say, or 'my MS makes me...' After accepting that we have the disease, we begin to take ownership of it. Because it is so different for everyone, there is no person who understands what the disease is to you, except you. My neurologist knows a lot, and continually learns more about MS; but he doesn't understand what my MS is. The people in my MS support group, who also suffer from the same disease, do not know what my MS is. My loving and supportive husband, though he tries to learn about Multiple Sclerosis, does not truly know my MS. We *met* my MS at the same time, and initially he became better acquainted with it than I did; however, once the exacerbations all subsided, he was not as close to my MS anymore, and is not as intimately familiar with it as I am. I hear him try to describe to other people some of my symptoms, and I am aware that he does not know my MS the way I thought he did. I try to keep it out of our lives as much as I can, so perhaps the fact that he doesn't know my MS as well as I thought he did means that I am successful.

It is a truly devastating, yet remarkably fascinating disease. There are many interesting facets to this disease. It can drastically change your life.

I plan for the worst, and hope for the best. We've all heard that, and everyone should follow that; but as a person living with MS, I have really grasped the importance of that phrase. I know there is a possibility that one day I may not be able to walk, see, climb stairs, drive, or type. To an extent, I plan my life accordingly. I don't let the disease rule my life, but some of my choices are based on the knowledge that I want to live for today. It's true that the same possibility exists for those without MS. Having this debilitating disease, which currently has no cure, brings that possibility a little closer.

One example of this is my recent automobile purchase. I had been driving the same vehicle for several years; as automobiles do when they get older, my Jeep Cherokee had more and more problems as time went on. My husband and I had kept planning to replace the Jeep, but through our past poor choices, we owed far too much on the Jeep, so trading it in had been postponed. I had changed my mind several times about what kind of car I wanted to get, but I was thinking sedan; something practical, a family car. It was about 6 months after my diagnosis that I really started researching cars on the internet; I was still looking at practical sedans. Then my 18 year old started talking to me about how inexpensive it would be for me to get a Mustang (one of my dream cars). I told him that I loved Mustangs but that I was looking for something more practical. But that got me thinking how many people don't get what they want because they think there is always time for that later; when the kids are grown, when I can afford to have an extra vehicle, when I retire, or whatever. I thought, "I have a disease that causes many people to become handicapped, and possibly end up having to give up driving. This disease is very unpredictable." So I decided it was time for a dream car. I checked, again on the internet, the local dealers; I looked at what colors and options were available in 2002 Mustangs. Then I chose the color and options that I wanted. The dealer nearest me didn't have the color I wanted, but I knew they could get it. I couldn't get that out of my mind, and one Thursday morning when I was out running errands, I decided to go have a look. The internet was correct, they didn't have it, but they could get the exact car that I wanted. It turned out *my Mustang* was 200 miles away, in Walla Walla. The dealership brought it up to Spokane for me. On Sunday afternoon, I drove it home. There were 300 miles on it, obviously 200 had been put on driving it to me. I love my silver 'Stang! Hopefully, the best will happen and I will be driving for the next 50 years (I'm 38 now), but if, God forbid, the worst happens, I have owned my dream car already, and that won't be one of my regrets!

There are actually some positives associated with being diagnosed with MS. Having Multiple Sclerosis gave me a new perspective; it truly impelled me to look at life differently. We all think we will take the time to do the things we've wanted to do next month, or next year, or when the kids graduate; when we have more time. After being diagnosed with MS, and knowing the impact that the MonSter could have on my life, I learned the importance of *taking* the time I had previously been *waiting* for. Those of us with MS, the Mighty Special people, really evaluate what is important to us in life. I make sure we spend family time doing the things we enjoy. My husband and I love golf. Having a couple of cellular stores, we get too busy to remember to enjoy ourselves at times. But golf is one of the things that I try harder to make sure we do. If my disease causes me to be unable to walk some day, I will also be unable to play golf. *Now* is the time to do the things I enjoy!

People don't know how to react when they find out you have MS. Most people don't even know what Multiple Sclerosis is. I've heard it said over and over that when someone hears the term Multiple Sclerosis they think of "Jerry's Kids." Muscular Dystrophy and Multiple Sclerosis are not even similar. That just goes to show how much people need to learn about both diseases.

You usually get one of two extremes from people in reaction to hearing that you have MS. Some people give you the "Oh, that's too bad." You never hear any reference to the disease from them again. You might as well have told them you have split ends or you broke a fingernail. Others act like you are going to die or something; every single time they see you they get this tone of concern (which, by the way, does not even feel genuine), touch your arm, and ask, "How are you doing?" These people are never able to carry on a conversation with you again. After their false concern, they move on to talk to someone else. It's like now that you have a disease, you're no longer worth talking to. Both extremes are hard to deal with. I feel like saying, "Hey, I have a disease that has taken over parts of my life; it's not killing me, it's just stealing from me." I don't want to ignore this MonSter, but I don't want to focus on it either. I don't want other people to ignore, or focus on it. I know it has to be difficult for those living on the outside to understand. All I ask is that they try…

Multiple Sclerosis hit me hard and fast in the beginning with no warning. Most people with MS have had symptoms, often minor but disturbing, for years and are relieved to finally have a diagnosis and a reason for feeling what they have been feeling. For others, like me, there is no leading up to the diagnosis. My first 'known' attack hit me hard starting in September of 2001 and lasted until sometime in late November or early December of 2001. I had my official diagnosis in January, 2002. It has been nine years now and the worst of it was in the beginning.

Haunted Romance

I woke up and looked around. Well, that's not exactly accurate. It's more that I suddenly became aware. I wasn't asleep; I was just not aware of my surroundings…well, of anything really. I didn't know what happened that brought me to be consciousness nor why I wasn't conscious in the first place. Nothing was familiar.

I could tell I was in a home; it wasn't my home though. It didn't seem to be a home I had ever been in. What if the owners didn't know me? I thought that I might have amnesia. This was the strangest thing that had ever happened in my life. I needed to think carefully and try to remember the last thing that had happened. When I tried to remember, suddenly my entire life started running through my mind, beginning with my birth.

Now that was very bizarre as I had no idea how I could remember my birth. Who has any memory of being born? It was so strange; it was like I was watching a movie of my entire life. I saw everything. But…wait a minute…how can that be? I saw myself getting old. Oh, no! I didn't understand any of this. This has to be the worst nightmare I've ever had. I've got to find a way to wake up! Perhaps I had been drugged. What sort of strange drug would cause me to feel this way?

Then I heard a key in the lock. I didn't want someone to walk in and find me in their house, but I thought it might wake my up. I didn't know what to think. I was losing my mind; I didn't know if I was having a horrible nightmare, or if I was just crazy. I needed to get control of myself. I would just explain that I apparently have amnesia and I don't know how I ended up here. Hopefully whoever lived here wouldn't freak out, or have me arrested, or shoot me.

The door opened and a young lady walked in. I figured I better announce myself immediately so she wouldn't think I was trying to hide, so I said, "I'm so sorry to surprise you this way but I honestly don't know where I am or how I ended up here and I don't mean to be in your home. This is all very odd and I'll be on my way. I didn't touch anything and once again I don't have any idea how I got here…" I suddenly realized two things; one of them was that I was rambling uncontrollably and the other was that the young lady right in front of me made no sign of hearing me. Oh, my, she must be deaf. I gently touched her arm, "Miss…"

She jumped and let out a scream as though she had been startled, grabbing her arm where I had touched her. She stood in one spot, her eyes wildly searching the room. "I didn't mean to startle you," I told her softly, and she made no sign of hearing me. I was standing directly in front of her, yet she didn't see me. Well, this was a problem, not only was she deaf, but she was also blind. Maybe I would just quietly sneak out of her house and she would never know I was here. I bent over to pick up her cardigan, which had been around her shoulders but fell to the floor when I startled her. I looked at her and she was wild eyed with fright. She was looking at the cardigan like she could see it but she couldn't see me. She screamed again.

That's when it occurred to me she couldn't see me because I was dead! When my life had run through my mind earlier, I had seen a body in a casket. That was my body. I was a ghost! Now I wished I was having a nightmare or some kind of weird drug induced hallucination. Why was I here? I didn't want to haunt anyone; and I certainly didn't want to haunt this lovely young lady. If I was indeed dead, I thought I would be on my way to heaven, where I would be greeted by my husband. This is definitely not what I thought it would be like to be dead.

The young lady who I was apparently supposed to 'haunt' was average height with long blonde hair. She was slender and obviously took care of herself. She was nice looking; not a stunner, but lovely in a sweet girl-next-door way. She seemed to have a timid personality, but I supposed that could be because of the things I had done that frightened her.

"Look, I don't want to scare you, sweetie. I am so confused about why I'm here," I started to say the woman, before remembering that she couldn't hear me. Without thinking, I picked up a pillow from the chair next to me. I saw the look on her face and quickly set it back down. The poor thing was shaking and I wanted to comfort her, but I knew she couldn't hear me and I wasn't about to touch her again. She sat down and put her head in her hands, softly sobbing.

Suddenly she sat up straight, shook her head and then stood up. "Get a grip on yourself," she seemed to be talking to herself. I could hear her just fine. Oh how I wished she could hear me. "You're imagining things...too much stress at work lately...maybe I should see a shrink...maybe I should stop talking to myself!" She laughed at herself and went about putting the groceries away that she had brought in with her.

I walked around her house while she put things away. I had no idea what I was supposed to do as a ghost, and I hoped this wasn't my eternal fate. The funny thing that I discovered was that I couldn't walk through walls. Maybe that would come later. I found that this young lady must live alone, and she was a very tidy person.

I heard her phone ring and decided to listen to her conversation, and I walked back to her kitchen. She was smiling as she talked, "I am planning to have dinner ready about 7 but feel free to come sooner, Kevin. I hope you like pasta." She seemed to be listening to 'Kevin' and then said, "I'll see you then, good-bye." I thought it was nice that she was going to have company, a beau! It sounded like it wasn't a steady boyfriend since she didn't know whether he liked pasta or not. I would have liked to have helped her with dinner. I always loved to cook.

I sat on one of the stools next to the counter and watched as she boiled the pasta and cut up vegetables for a salad. She reached over to turn on a radio and started singing along with the song. All of a sudden it occurred to me that I was invading her privacy. This poor young thing thought she was alone. Well, there wasn't anything I could do about it, so I had no reason to feel guilty; still, I couldn't help myself. She had just added the alfredo sauce to the fettuccini, along with some scallops, when the doorbell sounded. I followed her to the front door; again, I felt like it was none of my business but there was nothing else for me to do.

She opened the door, and there was a nice looking young man standing there looking rather nervous. "Hi Julie, I brought some wine to go with dinner. I hope you like Riesling. I got that movie you mentioned too."

At last! I had been wondering what her name was.

Julie stepped aside for Kevin to come in. "Come in, Kevin. Yes, Riesling will be perfect with what I made for dinner."

They were both so shy, but they looked cute together. I watched them throughout their meal, and they were both so formal and polite, and extremely shy, that I wondered if their relationship would ever progress into a romance, or if they would just be friends, as it seemed they would by their manner. Since I could not only hear their voices, but also their thoughts, it was obvious that they had a lot in common, were well suited and were crazy about each other but they were just too shy to vocalize it, or to show it. It was also apparent that they had known each other for quite some time and had been acting in this manner toward each other for almost as long as they had known each other and would probably continue in the same fashion.

After they finished eating, Kevin poured another glass of wine for each of them, while Julie rinsed the dishes and tidied up the kitchen. She turned around, "Do you want to watch the movie now?"

"Sure. I poured another glass of wine for you," Kevin said as he handed one of the glasses to her.

I occurred to me that these nice young people needed my help to advance in their relationship. I wasn't sure how I could do that, since I wouldn't be able to talk to them, but I knew that it would come to me as I was a very successful matchmaker my entire life. That's when I realized that this might be why I was here.

"I'll put the movie in," Kevin said, as Julie sat at one end of the sofa. He then walked back across the room and sat at the other end.

Oh for crying out loud, I felt like screaming! It was like they were afraid of each other. I knew what I had to do!

The movie started. It was a comedy. This would probably be easier if they had chosen a suspense or horror movie. They both set their wine glasses on the coffee table, and while they were engrossed in the movie, I slowly, so as not to let them see, moved their wine glasses closer together so that they were touching. My next move was to move the remote out of their reach and I pressed the "pause" button. I know what you're thinking; that's not scary. The idea was to start slow and subtle.

"What the heck?" Kevin exclaimed.

"Where did the remote go?" Julie stood up to look for it, finding it on the end table next to the rocking chair. "That's strange. I always leave the remote on the coffee table." As she was about to press the button to un-pause the movie, she noticed the wine glasses, "Kevin, did you move our glasses?'

"No," he said, and picked his glass up.

While, Julie had been retrieving the remote, I moved several throw pillows to her end of the sofa. Thinking Kevin had moved the pillows, Julie moved them to the center and sat at the end, wishing she had left them where they were. She was too shy to move them back. They went back to watching the movie.

I knocked on the front door. They both assumed there was someone outside and Kevin paused the movie while Julie got up to open the door. Of course, there was nobody there. Julie walked out onto the step and looked both ways before coming back in, "How weird," she said, closing the door, "there was nobody there."

"Huh," Kevin started the movie again.

As soon as Julie was seated, I knocked on the door again. Julie and Kevin looked at each other and they both got up to walk to the door. Kevin opened the door and I moved throw pillows onto both ends of the sofa. They both stepped outside and looked around. Kevin said, "It must be kids playing a practical joke."

After closing the door, Kevin said, "Let's wait by the door and see if they knock again, and we can open the door as soon as they do."

I picked up the remote and started the movie playing again. "What is going on with the movie? First it pauses on its own and then it starts playing on its own. Maybe I need a new DVD player," Julie stated. I decided I better pick up the pace. They were rationalizing everything I did.

I turned on the radio in the living room and then ran into the kitchen and turned on the radio there. I came back to the living room and turned the light switch on and off. Leaving the lights off, I walked over to the coffee table and picked up the remote, paused the movie and then started it and turned the volume up and down pressing the 'fast forward' button. They were both standing in the dark, with their jaws dropped.

I flipped the light switch on and off again, leaving it on this time so they could see. I knocked on the front door and then started knocking on the windows. Next I picked up a book from the end table and carried it across the room, setting it on the coffee table and picked up their wine glasses. Carrying the wine glasses, I set them on the table next to the door. Standing behind Julie, I lifted her hair and started blowing on her neck.

Julie screamed and ran into Kevin's arms. Finally! I turned the radios off and stopped the movie, and made no more moves. The two of them stood in each other's arms for several minutes and everything was quiet. After a few minutes Kevin said, "I don't know what just happened, but I'm kind of glad it did."

Julie nodded in agreement, tipping her head up to look at Kevin. His lips met hers, and they finally shared their first kiss.

My job was done. That was easy!

A Prayer for Christmas

It was Christmas Eve morning. Amber was pregnant with twins and was scheduled for a C-section in a month. Amber and Adam were keeping things quiet this Christmas. Instead of spending Christmas with their families, where things were always hectic, they were staying home and having only a few people over at a time. They were expecting Amber's parents to come over for brunch later, and Adam's parents would come in the afternoon. Their plans for Christmas Day were to have a quiet day at home.

Amber's pregnancy had been high risk and her doctor had ordered her to bed rest for the last two months. She felt like she was going stir crazy, but she was halfway through her bed rest and the reward would be their babies, a boy and a girl. They would have their perfect family, and they were grateful for that as the doctor had recommended that Amber not try to have any more pregnancies.

Adam made tea and brought it to Amber along with some fruit, and they spent a relaxing morning in bed watching "It's a Wonderful Life" on TV. Amber's mother had offered to bring a quiche over for their brunch and they arrived shortly after the movie was over. Adam went downstairs to help his in-laws bring in their things from the car. The three of them had just closed the door when they heard Amber scream and they ran upstairs, Adam leading three steps at a time.

"My water broke," Amber cried. "I've been so careful. Why did this happen?!"

Adam rushed to her side, putting his arms around her, "Don't worry sweetheart, everything will be fine. I'll call Dr. Baxter and we'll go right to the hospital. I'll help you get changed as soon as I call the doctor." Amber's parents, Evan and Margo, were amazed at how well Adam handled everything.

Margo and Adam assisted Amber in preparing to leave to the hospital, while Evan stayed out of the way, hoping he wouldn't be required to do anything. When it came time to help Amber to the car, Evan was happy to step in and help Adam with getting his daughter safely in the vehicle. Margo turned off the oven and the lights, locking the door before they stopped for a moment to say a prayer for Amber, the babies, and the doctor who would be performing the Caesarean, that the babies would be healthy, the c-section would go smoothly, and the doctor would have a steady hand. Then they all headed to the hospital.

The first baby, Noelle, had been delivered without incident, but they had been concerned about not finding the heartbeat of the boy. The doctor had explained when they hooked up the fetal monitor, "Sometimes with twins, one baby is behind the other and it's difficult or even impossible to detect the heartbeat." That had abated Amber's anxiety, but Adam had to work at not showing his distress. They were so excited over the birth of tiny Noelle it took their minds off her brother momentarily.

When they looked back to the doctor, though, the look on his face brought them back to reality. As he removed Christian, as they had decided to name him, from the uterus, he looked at Amber and shook his head, "I'm sorry. He is not breathing. We'll do everything we can." They took him away and it seemed like a lifetime to the young couple waiting to hear news on their baby. As a team worked on the baby, Amber's abdomen was sutured, although she seemed completely unaware.

When Dr. Baxter finally came back, it was without Christian. "I'm sorry we weren't able to get a heartbeat. We've tried longer than we probably should have, but we didn't want to give up on him."

"Can't you just try again?" Amber cried out. "Don't give up on my baby!"

"I'm sorry, Amber, I really am. We didn't have a heartbeat on him when you first got here. It's not going to help."

Adam felt like pleading for them to keep trying also, but he was also concerned for his wife. The logical part of him told him to try to sooth her.

"Can we see him?"

"Of course, the nurse will bring him over, and we'll leave you with him for as long as you need."

Amber was crying uncontrollably when the nurse brought their lifeless infant to them, wrapped in a blanket, laying him across Amber's chest. Adam held his wife's hand with one of his, and laid his other hand on Christian's chest, "Father in Heaven, please don't let our baby be dead. Bring him back to us, Lord. Please, God, please..." Adam was now crying too hard to continue his prayer out loud. He cradled little Christian in his arms, sobbing quietly.

Amber softly laid her hand on Adam's arm, "Adam? I need to see Christian. Please take him from the blanket and lay him on my chest."

Amber held her blanket up to allow Adam to lay the baby on her bare chest. Adam laid his arm across both his wife and their dead baby protectively. Amber started to sing a lullaby to Christian. They were still in that position when the doctor came into the room.

Adam looked at the doctor, "We're not ready." The doctor walked back out.

"He feels so soft and warm," Amber said. "Adam, take your shirt off and lay with us." Adam did as his wife requested and she continued to sing. Suddenly they both felt his fingers move slightly. "Adam, they were wrong! Christian is alive!"

A nurse came in trying not to disturb them and picked up a chart. She was just opening the door to leave when Adam said, "Nurse, there's been a mistake. Our baby is still alive. He's moving his fingers."

The nurse looked at him doubtfully, "I'll get Dr. Baxter for you." She left the room. It was almost fifteen minutes later when the doctor came into the room.

He looked at the couple sadly and said, "I know this is hard, and I'm not going to say that I know what you're going through because I have never experienced this from your side. It is common for the deceased to have some movements occasionally. I can assure you it is just reflexes." He was pulling his stethoscope from his pocket and listening as he said this. The doctor listened, moved the stethoscope slightly and listened again before shaking his head, "No, I'm sorry, there is no heartbeat. I'll give you some more time." With that he walked out the door. He didn't mean to appear cold, but he didn't want to give them false hope.

Amber and Adam looked into each other's eyes and then at their tiny boy. Amber shook her head, "He's wrong, Adam. I know Christian is alive." They laid there and held their baby singing and stroking his little body. From time to time, a nurse would poke her head in the door and leave quietly.

They didn't know how long they had been lying on that hospital bed when Amber saw Christian's eyes start to twitch. "Adam, look at Christian's face." They both looked at their son as his eyes opened slightly, blinking slowly. A nurse poked her head in the door just then and Amber said, "Get Dr. Baxter! My baby is alive."

When the grandparents were allowed to visit briefly on Christmas Day, Amber and Adam led them to the nursery where they were able to see both their granddaughter and their grandson, unbelievably small, incredibly precious and hooked up to IVs and in their incubators. All of their Christmas prayers had been answered.

A Prayer for Christmas is based on a touching story I heard on the news one evening.

Finding Us

I pulled into my garage, turned off the engine and opened my trunk to get my grocery bags out. I was glad that the next day would be Friday. It had been a long week and I was looking forward to a relaxing weekend. Setting one of the bags on the garage floor, I unlocked the door and picked the bag up again. Just as I was walking into the kitchen my phone rang. I knew it would be Linda, inviting me once again to go out for dinner and drinks after work on Friday. I almost always turned her down and yet she kept inviting me. I suppose I was glad that she didn't give up on me. I had divorced my husband almost a year before and Linda was constantly encouraging me to socialize more. She was probably right, I probably should be getting out more, but I was completely comfortable with how my life was going now.

I looked at the caller ID as I picked up the phone, "Hi Linda."

"Meg, is this a good time to talk?"

"I just walked in the door with my groceries. I can talk while I put things away. What's up?" I don't know why I asked since I knew why she was calling.

"Rachel suggested going to dinner at the casino tomorrow night and then we can try to strike it rich playing some games. What do you think?"

I sighed, "I don't think so, Linda, I've got lots to do this weekend and I don't want to start Saturday out being tired. Thank you for thinking of me though."

"Meg, you can't just stay home all the time. I don't care if you date anyone, but you can't spend the rest of your life being a homebody. You could just come for dinner and if you don't want to gamble, you can go home after we eat. How 'bout it? You have to eat anyway and the seafood buffet is to die for."

By this time I had finished putting my groceries away and was stuffing my canvas shopping bag in the drawer, "All right, Linda, I'll come to dinner. But I'll take my own car so I can drive home after we eat."

I could almost sense Linda's surprise that I had agreed. "Oh, I'm so glad! We'll have fun! Rachel and Julie will be glad that you're joining us. I'll see you tomorrow!"

I hung up the phone and opened a can of soup to heat up for my dinner. I rarely cooked a full meal anymore, usually just opening a can of soup. It seemed silly to spend the time cooking when it was just me. Phil and I had split after being married for just over five years. We both realized that we had married for all the wrong reasons and we ruined a good friendship by getting married. Our divorce had been somewhat amicable but we never talked anymore. Thankfully we didn't have any children during our marriage. There are enough kids from broken homes in the world; I certainly didn't want to add to that.

After ladling some soup in a bowl, I poured a glass of wine and set both on my desk next to my laptop and turned it on. I was probably spending too much time on Facebook, but I was enjoying getting back in touch with so many of my friends from the past. I logged on and noticed I had two friend requests. The first one was my cousin, Justine. I was pleased she had found me; she and I had been so close when we were growing up. Justine was a year older than me and had gone to college in Texas and stayed there following graduation. We only saw each other occasionally at family events now. It would be nice to catch up with her. When I saw the name of the other person I nearly dropped my wine glass. Will Gibson! I hadn't seen Will in years, but thought about him often. Will and I had dated almost all the way through high school, and we'd known each other since kindergarten. Everyone had been so sure we would get married. I think Will and I thought so as well.

I accepted both friend requests and my heart started fluttering at the thought of reconnecting with Will. What was wrong with me? I am a grown woman and Will is probably married. It would just be nice to catch up and find out what had been going on in his life for the past decade. Will probably lived on the other side of the country, or maybe he didn't even live in this country. We had both graduated from high school in Bellingham. Will had joined the Air Force and I went to Western Washington University. I had never left Whatcom County. Our ten year class reunion was coming up next year. Ever since my divorce, I had fantasized about meeting up with Will at the reunion and rekindling our romance. His friend request was bringing these fantasies of renewing our relationship back to my mind. Stop it, Meg, I chastised myself for being so silly! I promised myself to change my thinking. I finished up on my computer and logged off. I really did need to get my addiction to Facebook under control. It seriously wouldn't kill me to go a day without logging on!

I loaded my few dishes into the dishwasher and started a load of laundry. Since I planned to paint the kitchen over the weekend I decided to get a head start and cleared everything off the shelves and counters, putting everything in boxes. I had chosen a soft yellow for my kitchen walls, with a warm mocha trim. I always wanted yellow in my kitchen but my ex-husband argued against it. Yellow is so cheerful and I was looking forward to brightening up the walls. I don't know what took me so long to make this change. The buzzer on the dryer alerted me that my clothes were dry just as I finished setting the last box on the living room floor.

I woke up Saturday morning feeling tired but actually kind of glad that I had gone out with my friends the night before. Usually I only feel regret about being talked into staying out after dinner; the few times it had happened anyway. We had gambled a bit and I actually had come out a little over a hundred dollars ahead for the evening. I was surprised that I had so much fun. Perhaps it was time for me to start circulating again as Linda kept telling me.

After a quick shower, I dressed in jeans and a t-shirt, pulled on a jacket and headed to the store to pick up the paint. I had agonized over the color samples for months before choosing the shade of yellow I wanted. I hoped I wouldn't be disappointed once I got home with it or more importantly after it was on my wall.

I decided to get a latte and a bagel before going home. I knew that once I started painting I wouldn't stop to eat until I was done. Carrying the paint, brushes and everything into the house I figured I would log onto Facebook while I ate my bagel and realized that the last time I was on Facebook was Thursday evening. There were a few new messages. I opened the first one which was a message from my cousin, Justine, who told me how glad she was that we were able to connect on Facebook. She was planning to come to Bellingham in a couple of months and hoped we could spend some time catching up while she was in town. I quickly responded to her message and told her I too was glad to reconnect and was looking forward to seeing her when she was in town.

The next message was about the ten year class reunion which was coming up too soon. It was so hard to believe that ten years had passed so quickly. I found myself wishing I had accomplished more in that time.

The final message was from Will. I opened his message and saw that he was in town and had sent me the message to invite me to dinner last night. I felt disappointed that hadn't gotten the message in time, but as I read further it seemed that Will would be in town a bit longer. Just as I was about to respond to the message, the 'chat' popped up in the lower right.

"Hey Meggie! Glad 2 c ur on. Did u get my message?"

I hesitated, not quite knowing what to say. "Hi Will," was all I typed.

"I wanted 2 take u 2 dinner last nite guess u didn't get my message."

"I haven't been on FB since Thursday night."

"I'm in town til next Thursday hope we can hook up"

"That would be nice."

"R u busy 2day?"

"Actually I am. I'm painting my kitchen today." Meg always used proper spelling, grammar, punctuation and such on Facebook even though most everyone else she knew didn't.

"What about 2nite?"

"I don't think I will feel up to it tonight, Will. Why don't we have lunch tomorrow if you're not busy?"

"Was hoping 2 c u sooner but that worx what's ur #"

I typed in my cell phone number.

"y don't I help u paint"

I paused. I wanted to see Will, but I didn't think it was a good idea to have him paint my kitchen the first time we saw each other in almost ten years. "Thanks, but I really would rather do it myself. I appreciate the offer though. I really should get to work now. See you tomorrow."

"K. I will call u later 2 c where u want 2 go & what time 4 lunch"

"Bye Will. I'm looking forward to seeing you."

I logged off, turned up the music and started painting. I was a little surprised to notice how my mood had lifted after talking to Will. He had always made me smile, even when we were little kids. After painting a bit, I stood back from the wall and was really pleased with the color. It was exactly what I had pictured. My kitchen would be the cheery center of the house I had always wanted it to be.

As I turned back to painting, I was in the best mood I had been in more than a year. The combination of the fabulous color I was applying to the walls, the great music on the radio, and talking to my old beau had put me in such a good mood that I finished painting much sooner that I thought would. I realized that I wanted to have new towels and potholders to compliment the walls.

After showering to get the paint out of my hair and off my fingers and arms I quickly dressed and drove to Bed Bath & Beyond to find some things to accessorize my "new" kitchen. When I got home and put my new items in the kitchen as well as replacing the things I had moved out I was very pleased with the result.

Hunger was starting to nag at me and I realized I hadn't eaten lunch. It was now after seven so I made myself a salad. As I was sitting down to eat my cell phone rang. I thought it must be Will and I suddenly felt nervous.

"Hey Meggie!"

"Hi Will! How are you?"

"I'm good, but I'll be better when I get to see you."

"I'm looking forward to seeing you too, Will."

"Have you given any thought to where you want to eat?" Will asked.

"There's a new café with a great view of Bellingham Bay. They have excellent food and the service is excellent. How does that sound?"

"Sounds great to me, Meg. I'll pick you up at noon if that works for you. I'll just need your address. I think I still know my way around." I gave Will my address and we talked for about twenty minutes more before saying our good-byes and hanging up.

My door bell rang exactly at noon. I opened the door to see Will standing there holding out a beautiful bouquet of daisies, white mini carnations and yellow tulips. "Oh Will, these are so nice and will look perfect in my kitchen with the new paint. Thank you!"

He smiled, "I remember how you always loved yellow. You used to say it was the happiest color."

I was surprised Will remembered that. I smiled back at him and stood on my tip toes to kiss his cheek and give him a hug. I put the flowers in water and set them on the kitchen counter.

"You're kitchen looks great, Meg! It's so cheerful."

I smiled, "Thank you, Will, I think so too."

We headed down to the waterfront and walked into the café.

"I heard about your divorce, Meg. I'm really sorry," Will said after we found our seats.

I shook my head, "Don't be, Will. It just wasn't meant to be. Phil and I ruined a good friendship by getting married. We never had any children so I'm glad for that. What about you? Did you get married?" I glanced at his left hand as I asked, wondering why I hadn't looked before now.

"Yah, I got married a few years ago, but she was immature and decided she didn't want a husband in the service so we weren't even married a year when she filed for divorce. No kids for us either."

"I'm really glad you found me on Facebook, Will," I said, smiling. He smiled back.

We sat silently for a few moments and looked into each other's eyes, "What ever happened to us, Meg?" Will asked.

"We were just kids, Will. We had to experience life. I don't think we even broke up. We just drifted apart. Time and distance got in our way and life happened to us in the meantime."

He nodded, "I think you're right, Meg."

We talked for a long time. Other patrons came and went and we didn't pay any attention to any of them until a waiter came by our table for the fourth time asking if we needed anything else.

"We should clear out and let them have their table. Do you want to walk along the waterfront?"

I agreed with Will and we walked and talked for hours. We talked about everything that had happened in our lives in the seven or eight years since we had seen each other last.

I found out that Will had recently been stationed at McChord Air Force Base and would be out in a year. "I decided to spend my leave in Bellingham to help me decide whether to move back here after I'm out of the Air Force."

"Really? That would be fantastic," I said, enthusiastically.

I shivered and we realized the sun was setting. "You're cold and it's getting late. Why don't I buy you dinner?" Will asked as he put his arm around me.

I was enjoying the time with Will too much to say anything but yes to his invitation. I was so comfortable with him and it had been as if we had not been separated by miles and years as soon as we had started talking that day. We had a nice dinner at a seafood restaurant that we had gone to on special occasions back in high school. It was a delightful evening and when Will dropped me off at my house we made plans for dinner the next night.

Will and I had dinner together for the next three evenings. "I have to go back to McChord tomorrow. I've gotten used to having dinner with you. I'll miss you," Will told me as we were eating dinner at my house the last night he was in town.

I touched his hand and said, "I'm going to miss you too, Will. I've really enjoyed spending time with you."

He looked into my eyes, "If you don't mind, I think I'll be coming to Bellingham every chance I get."

"Mind? I'll be mad if you don't come visit me."

It was at that point that we kissed. It was reminiscent of the kisses we used to share, but oh, so much better.

For the next year, Will came to Bellingham whenever he could and I went to Tacoma whenever I could. We spent weekends and Holidays together and made up for all the years apart. Will moved to Bellingham after leaving the Air Force just two weeks before our 10 year high school reunion and moved in with me.

The first night Will shared my house we went out to dinner and walked along the waterfront afterward. Suddenly Will stopped walking, turned to face me, taking my hands in his and went down on one knee, "Meg, you were my best friend in high school and I lost you. I was so happy to find you again, and even happier that you were willing to spend time with me. I don't ever want to lose my best friend again. When we were high school sweethearts you were the cutest girl in school; now you're the most beautiful woman I have ever seen. I love you so much. This past year has been amazing, sharing everything we have shared. I want to share the rest of my life with you. Please make me the happiest man in the world and agree to be my wife."

I started shaking as soon as Will took my hands. I should have seen it coming but I was completely surprised by Will's proposal. Before I could answer, he took a ring box from his pocket, opened it and displayed before me was the most beautiful diamond ring I had ever seen. I started to cry.

"Oh, Will! Of course I will marry you!"

"I was happy when I found you on Facebook. I'm ecstatic that we found us!"

The kiss we shared then was amazing; complete with fireworks and everything. I had been worried about not having anything interesting to tell my former classmates at the reunion. Now I would be able to tell everyone the wonderful story about Will and me finding us!

One Last Thing...

I love to cook, and I love to share my favorite recipes. I'm always looking or recipes for light dishes that are good for you and are full of flavor. The recipe I chose to include in this book is a delicious pasta with shrimp and garlic. If you don't like shrimp, I've thought of using scallops, or even mushrooms, instead. I use more garlic than the recipe calls for and also a little more baby spinach leaves.

Garlic Shrimp Pasta

Ingedients

8 oz uncooked mulitgrain angel hair pasta
4 cups fresh baby spinach leaves
1 1/2 cups halved cherry tomatoes
3 teaspoons olive oil
1 medium onion, finely chopped (1/2 cup)
1 1/2 lb. medium shrimp, peeled, deveined and tail shells removed
3 cloves garlic, finely chopped
1/4 teaspoon crushed red pepper flakes
1/2 cup dry white wine (or chicken broth)
1/4 cup chicken broth
1/4 teaspoon salt
1/8 teaspoon pepper
3 tablespoons choppped fresh parsley
2 tablespoons butter

Method

1. In 5 quart saucepan cook pasta as directed on package. Drain, return to saucepan. Stir in spinach, tomatoes and 2 tablespoons of the oil. Cover to keep warm.

2. While pasta is cooking, in 12 inch non-stick skillet, heat remaining 1 teaspoon of olive oil over medium high heat. Add onion, cook and stir 1 minute. Add shrimp, garlic and red pepper flakes, cook and stir 2 minutes.

3. Stir in wine, broth, salt and pepper, cook 2 minutes or until shrimp are pink and firm. Remove from heat, stir in parsley and butter until butter is melted. Add shrimp mixture to pasta mixture in saucepan, toss to mix.

Enjoy!

Made in the USA
Lexington, KY
13 July 2012